"Draw near me—I must tell you something strange and rather fearsome, and I would take your hand in mine . . ."

I went and knelt beside him before the fire, and held his hand. He smiled down at me, and his black eyes were unfaded and proud as he said, "Only in times of peril do we burden our younglings with this old and bitter secret. Yet there is in this strange thing aid for all of the house of Raithe. Those Who Wait, those ghosts whom you hear on the wind and feel in the chill of your bones, those waiting ones are . . . were . . . of our blood. They are those of our house who fell in wrath upon this land, in this house, defending their own from those rapacious ones who ever seem to be spawning in the out-world . . ." He paused at my gasp of comprehension. "And they are kindly disposed to us who are their distant children. One who flees for life across the wildlands may find guidance in their cries. Your grandam and I were the last to follow them to safety. We had hoped to be the last ever to take that dark road. But, should you be driven forth, follow them if they call to you. Follow them . . . follow them . . ." And he seemed to drift again into his dark dream.

HOW THE GODS WOVE IN KYRANNON

by

ARDATH MAYHAR

SF

ace books

A Division of Charter Communications Inc.
A GROSSET & DUNLAP COMPANY
51 Madison Avenue
New York, New York 10010

An ACE Book

First Mass Market Edition
Published by arrangement with Doubleday & Co. Inc.

First Ace printing: February 1982
Published Simultaneously in Canada
2 4 6 8 0 9 7 5 3 1
Manufactured in the United States of America

Part I:

The Warp Is Set

The Hunting

Where the silver-foliaged forests swept in their wide arc between mountains, beside a stream that chattered between ferned banks, stood a stone house so old that its weathered walls seemed a part of the wood and the turf. The ancient moon-trees of the forest bent above the mossy roof and dropped web-soft leaves on the porches and the paths. They made a gray carpet where the feet of Cara passed about her tasks, and they whispered down the roof when the rains of fall began.

As season followed season, no change touched the house, or the wood, or the woman who lived there; for Tisha the Wise was slender and gray-clad and quiet-footed, as she had been for long and would be. But the years made great changes in the youngling who grew from child to woman. And Cara, no longer a child, began to dream of a world which must lie beyond the murmurous trees and the patient mountains.

"The world has been and will be," said Tisha sharply, when queried. "When you have learned the secrets of the earth and the wood and the Wildings in the secret places, then you will have reason to look afar toward other mysteries. Do you yet understand the working of the seed you tuck into the garden soil? Can you look through the eyes of your little cat, to see the world as she sees? Until you have spoken with the People of the Heights in mutual trust, or with a Wilding in his cool fastness, do not seek to meddle with the world beyond the mountains."

"Yet I know that you have walked in the places over-mountain," cried Cara, rebelliously. "It did you no harm, and you surely learned much!"

"Aye, I learned," chuckled Tisha, narrowing her gray eyes as if against a light. "No harm? Perhaps, but no good, either, did it do for me. I learned to distrust all who dwelt beneath roofs. I learned to fear, and that is no light lesson. I saw beauty to make the eye start from its socket, coupled with cruelty that would astonish a wolf in the hills. And, having seen your fine world, sought out a finer place, suited to the life of a thinker and watcher and healer. Here, where my far grandsirs dwelt, I brought you, my child-in-heart, that you might grow unwarped by the terrible stresses of the world of men."

Cara leaned toward her mother and touched her sleeve. The light of anger died from her eyes, and she said softly, "How came we here? Never have you talked with me of our journey and its cause, or of my father, or of the thing that drove you into the wild."

"Have never does not mean will never," said Tisha, catching up a basket. "But now the nuts litter the ground beneath the brownnut trees, and our winter store is not made. Come to the forest and forget your unease for now. Fall is no time for the heart to wander."

They went out into the scented winds that whipped their cloaks about their bodies and swept the pain from their tight hearts. Through the apple orchard they walked, stopping now and again to claim a windfall neglected when they harvested their crop. The crisp mellowness of the fruit lay on their tongues like a blessing, and they looked with gladness into the flying cloud-wrack above them, feeling the season possess their beings through all senses.

"This is a good world," admitted Cara as they entered the narrow track their feet had worn, year after year, through the lofty forest on the way to the nutwood. The web-gray leaves cushioned their steps, and the silver skin of the trees glimmered with a light like the moon behind cloud. A Grack watched them solemnly from his perch on a high branch, bending his short neck and cocking his round black head, following their progress as they walked beneath him, until he was peering upside-down beneath the tree limb. Then Cara laughed aloud, walking backward on tiptoe in order to see his glossy tail anchored desperately on the near side of the branch.

As if suddenly realizing his undignified position, the bird righted himself and gazed into the wood, ignoring them completely. Then Tisha joined in the mirth, and mother and daughter went down the path in a chime of laughter.

They found the nutwood awash with wealth for squirrel and bird and humankind, though but they two wore the form of man; and before the afternoon was spent, the women had filled their baskets and their bags. Then they sat upon a stone, talking, watching their companions at their garnerings, and enjoying the spicy scent of the brownnut trees.

Then there came a sort of hush among the creatures

gleaning among the leaves. Another Grack, just visible on a far limb, seemed to be observing some traveler on the path. Tisha stood then and said, "One comes, and no man or beast, I think. A Wilding? Let me see . . ." And she closed her eyes for a space of two heartbeats, seeming to fold into herself. "A Wilding," she repeated positively. "And in pain. Come, Cara, gather up our store and follow, for there is need of a healer—and perhaps more than a healer."

They hurried toward the path, burdened with their brownnuts, yet making all haste. No sound of footsteps guided them toward the newcomer; only Tisha's sensing told her where he walked. Unerringly, she moved through the trees, along the path. It was not long until she spied the Wilding, who had stopped and was resting against a moon-tree, nursing his side and breathing in controlled gasps which told of severe pain.

"Ho, wood-brother!" cried Tisha, setting down her burden and moving to his side. "You have great need of a healer, I fear. How came you in this state?" She moved his hands aside to see the wound, then gasped in shock as the ragged slash appeared.

Cara hurried to them and knelt amid the leaves. "This is the wound of no weapon of the wood-people!" she said. "What nature of being assaults one of these gentle folk with such?"

"Those who dwell in the 'world,'" answered her mother, with a bitter twist to her lips. "Is it not so?" she asked the Wilding.

He opened his long golden eyes, which glowed strangely in his umber-colored face, and the mane of short silver hair rippled upon the back of his neck as he said, in a faraway, whispering voice, "So it was, Lady. A man from beyond the highlands, it must be, hunted us as we walked in the deep dells, gathering our winter fare. My mate and our young concealed themselves and I ran, keeping him after me, but I slipped among the mossy stones. Then he stood above me and flung the spear he carried. It was only the kindness of the gods that sent it wide of the mark, else it would have sunk into my heart." He gasped and closed his eyes as Tisha bound him tightly with a length torn from her robe.

"Come to our house, that we my tend this wound. Nay, I know you dislike roofs, and I will not ask that you remain beneath mine—only that you come, so that I may use my lotions and balms upon this ugly cut."

The Wilding had started at mention of the house, but he calmed and nodded. The two women assisted him to walk, not forgetting their store of provender. The Grack was astonished to see two of humankind leading a Wilding, and he peered so interestedly that he well-nigh lost his balance upon his perch and was forced to flap his ebony wings desperately in order to remain aloft. Then, despite pain and anxiety, the three whom he watched laughed together and went on their way with lighter hearts.

The wound was soon cleaned and tended, and the Wilding consented to eat beneath their roof, which was a great concession from one of his kind. And strange did he look indeed, with his cunningly knotted fiber cloak and kilt draped upon his lithe and earth-toned frame, sitting within the frame of a firelit room, surrounded by all the artifacts of man. The light ran rampant through his silver hair, making it seem to burn upward in a close cap, then stream in its roached ridge down his spine to the shoulder. Yet his ways were easy and his manners unembarrassed.

Cara smiled as she moved back and forth in the firelight, watching her mother and the Wilding as they talked. So unlike were they in appearance and bearing that it was instantly apparent that they were of differing species; yet so similar were their inner selves that their kinship seemed to glow through the cloaking flesh. They seemed, to her knowing eye, two twilit creatures of the quiet places, soft and gentle to look upon, but steely in their inner strength.

As she watched, Tisha leaned forward and laid her slender hand upon that of the Wilding. He started, his strong ivory-colored digging claws appearing and retracting as a reflex. But she spoke quietly to him and he smiled and relaxed in the chair. The air of tension went from him.

"You might even come to like a roof," teased Tisha, as she saw this. "Yet all to their own ways. The problem we must now solve is this: what one among humankind is walking our forested hills with death in his heart for those unlike himself? This concerns more than your people, Loor, for the People of the Heights are also unlike. Even we, human though we be, are utterly unlike, beneath our skins, and might well run afoul of this killer-for-pleasure. What manner of man was he to look upon?"

Loor's eyes seemed to turn inward, as he looked again upon that figure. "Not over-tall was he," he said at last.

"Far below the height of our kind. His hair was dark as old moss upon a stone, and it was cut short below his ears. His eyes were two holes into darkness. He was clad in the way of men—richly, it seemed to me. But you will know him by his smile. He laughs when he kills. Aye, he laughs . . ." And Loor spoke no more.

The woman nodded slowly, her hand beneath her rounded chin, her gray eyes narrowed as if she looked into the past. Long she sat in silence, until Loor shook himself and stood.

"Far must I go to reach my own," he said, touching the sleeve of Tisha's robe shyly. "Yet I must give you thanks for your aid. None other is there upon this side of the mountains who can help those who need a healer. From henceforth you have only to call in the forest, if you have need. One of the People will hear you, however lonely the wood may seem, and I or one of mine will come." Then he was gone, leaving behind a gentle swirl of air and a faint scent of fernwood after rain.

Tisha drew a long sigh and her head bent into her hands. Cara came at once to kneel beside her. "How is it with you, my mother?" she asked.

"Well enough, Cara, yet this is just another such as was your father. One who laughs when he hurts, when he kills. And that, my dearest one, is the reason you and I sit here in the lap of the hills, girded round by forest."

"Did he hurt you?" asked Cara, her mouth stern.

"Not with whips nor with hands," her mother answered. "But with words, oh yes, and with fell deeds against man and beast and bird. I came from the garden one day and found him teaching you to beat my whimpering puppy. You were crying, and he looked as though he would next begin beating you. Then I knew that my father had made a marriage that I could not keep. That night I took you from your cradle and left the house and the town and the world that I knew, seeking only for a place which contained none of his kind. At last I found my way to the place of my fathers, and it sufficed."

"But all were not like him, surely," said Cara. "Were there no kindly folk who would aid and shelter you?"

"In your 'world,' youngling, men busy themselves with wealth and position and power, women with luxury and frivolity, in the main. The humble are fearful and the powerful callous. Had your father beaten us with whips there would have been aid—not otherwise."

They sat silent, hand in hand, for a time. Then Tisha stood decisively. "Let us to bed, for the morning will bring labors for us. We go to seek out this slayer of 'beasts,' wherever he now hunts. If he can be taught, we shall teach him. If not, I shall slay him."

Cara blanched. "But is this not the same carelessness of life that you fled?" she asked.

"Not carelessness, care," said her mother sternly. "Would you have the Wildings slaughtered until the forest reeks with the scent of rotting flesh? Would you have the hills and the woodpaths empty of life? Among all kinds, as well we know, there sometimes occur rogues that prey upon all that lives. Our unfortunate kind brings them forth with great regularity. You must understand that death is no terrible gift, but the wasting of life is sin.

The secret lies in knowing when to bestow the gift of death—whose life will spill into the earth as enrichment, not as waste.

"I was not ignorant when I went from my father's house in Lirith. Your grandparents were learned in the lore of mankind, mind and body, and the healing of both. I was trained as you have been, to set my hand with thoughtful care to whatever task the gods brought. Had my father not been far gone down the road to death, where he followed my mother, he would have seen into the heart of Ranith, your father, and would never have urged me to wed with him. Knowing this, I did not hesitate to break the bond my father forged, for his own teachings forbade me to continue in such a soul-destroying place as the one in which I found myself.

"Now I am no longer young and impulsive. What I do, I do after deep thought and in the service of the gods. Though my course may seem ruthless to you, tender as you are and inexperienced in the ways of our kind, yet remember that I have lived long and suffered much, but have not grown sour and hating. I am filled with pity for the man whom we shall hunt, yet I will do that which it is good to do, whatever it be."

Cara sat, gazing upward at the face of her mother. In the flickering light, it was still, as if cut from ivory, but from those gray eyes flashed utmost resolution, utmost courage. The girl sighed, then said, "You have wrested life from the wilderness these many years. You fled cruelty and are always just, with kindness a part of your spirit. You have taught me to weigh all things in the balance of my mind, then to judge. Thus I must find that you are most likely in the right, as much as mankind can be without a clear sign from the gods. I will go with you, and we will hunt this killer in the fastnesses. I shall aid you in whatever seems just."

So they turned to their couches and slept deeply.

The stone house dreamed under frosty stars, and the leaves drifted onto the roof, softly as snow. The moon-trees glimmered in the hills and the valleys, and in the gentle darkness slept Wilding and beast alike. But on a far outcrop of stone there shone a ruddy star of fire, and in its glow lay a man, propped against a pack, who sharpened a spear with a saw-toothed blade. The red light danced on the shaft and dripped like blood from the bright blade, lighting the quiet smile of pleasure on the face of the man as he drew the whetstone over the steel.

Night flowed over the rim of the world, and dawn followed on its heels. In the stone house, Tisha and her daughter donned stout clothing and footgear. Food they packed, and medicines, and they chose staffs with steel points to aid them should they need to ascend the heights.

The rising sun, peering pale and abstracted between flying wracks of cloud, found them upon the path. Single-file they walked, speaking little, but looking closely to the tracks in the trail, the forest on either hand, and stopping now and again to listen and to sense the air. Tisha stepped silently, her head slightly tilted, as a hart walks in its own place. Cara came behind, almost as silently, swinging her arms in pleasure at the physical action. Yet even to Cara's watchful eyes, the figure of her mother almost seemed to melt into the silver-gray motley of the wood. The girl was careful never to fall a pace behind or to let her attention stray too far.

So, when Tisha paused, at midmorning, to study the mix of prints in the damp leaf-mold of the trail, Cara was just behind.

"The Wildings have been abroad," whispered the woman. "Here are the prints of Leera, the mate of Loor. Do you remember, years ago, that she wrenched her foot awry amid the stones of the stream and came to me for aid? It left her lame, and here is her mark. The man walks in another direction than this, or Loor would surely have been with Leera. We must turn our steps to the east, toward the foothills. Pray that the People of the Heights be wary and avoid his path."

Across the valley floor, cloaked with thick forests, they went. Before night they saw the thinning of the woodlands and the rise of land that told them their nearness to the foothills. The sun, which had merely lit the clouds from above all the day, now peeped below the western edge of the gray mat and dyed the near ranges with bronze fires. Then the two hurried their pace and climbed rapidly into the folded lands, making for the ridge that lay before them. There they hunted out a dry burrow beneath a fallen trunk and, hiding all traces of their approach, went to earth. From their packs they drew down-filled mats backed with the hides of beasts, which made their bed, and they ate cold meat and fruit and drank sparingly of their water.

For a little time they lay, listening to the earth-sounds about them, well content to be there, for often they would go into the wild for pleasure and lay their heads where they willed for days or weeks. The tick of the beetle in the old wood that was their roof was as familiar a sound, and as friendly, as the crick-crack of the cooling fireplace in their house. The hunting owl moved in the stillness, and they felt the prowling wolf as he hunted. Far away and above, they heard soft, whooping cries, infinitely mournful in the stillness, that they knew to be those of the People of the Heights. They stiffened unconsciously, listening carefully, analyzing every nuance of those calls.

"They are not at rest," said Cara. "There might be many reasons, but my heart tells me there is only one. The man camps above."

Tisha turned to peer through the dead bracken, though nothing could be seen. "Aye, he is there. I feel him. I almost hear his thoughts. Red his fire and red his heart. We shall find him tomorrow, mayhap. He has no feeling that he is hunted, no warning from instinct. That is no gift brought by the towns of men. When you or I are sought, we know."

They lay side by side, breathing softly, feeling outward with their spirits, through the night. The small creatures they felt, and the large. The man lay asleep on the edge of their seeking.

"Strange," said Cara. "He has no feel of malice. There is no black wickedness there."

"No," said Tisha, with a sigh of relief. "He is not another such as your father. This is a youngling, little older than you, who has not learned the permanence of death. He sleeps as a child, dreaming of deeds of daring. Perhaps we need not slay after all."

Then they, too, slept, while the night swept soundlessly over them.

Again the rising sun found them on the move. They were near to the mountains now, and their path grew steep and stony. All the ways were known to them—even the secret paths of the People of the Heights—and those they followed into the high places.

"Now has the time come, my child, that you may speak with the People in their own places," said Tisha, as they climbed. "We must tell them of their danger and our mission, that they may lie safe and silent until the peril is past. They know you, as they know me, in our lowland forests, but they will be shy. Be wary, for they are determined folk and may well send a boulder upon us before they see us well. They have no seeking sense and must deal with the things they see."

No long while passed before they saw, upon an outcrop of rock high above them, a small gray figure which watched them closely. Then Tisha called, a low, whooping cry much like that which had pierced the night. The figure straightened, human-like and small against the sky, and its hand moved in a gesture which traced a symbol upon the air.

Up they moved, clambering over standing stones and finding their way, shoulder and foot, up chimneys weather-worn in the mountain's face. At last they stood at the top in a shallow saucer rimmed with tumbled rock. A group of the People awaited them there, standing quietly, their silken-smooth gray fur ruffled by the damp wind, their squat bodies still, and their round faces quiet, save for the watchfulness of their eyes.

Long had it been since one of the People had sought them out, and Cara had forgotten the strangeness of those eyes, which were as panes of glass which looked inward upon a world of untroubled blue. No ripple touched those eyes, and now all those many windows were turned upon them. Tisha made the sign of peace and friendship and sat upon a stone, whereupon all came near and sat, also.

The language of the People was strange: a soft twittering at times, with sad little hoots and cries interspersed with whispering sibilances. No man could learn it well, but Tisha had managed after a fashion, and she spoke with him who had awaited them.

Long they talked, Wheesha (as nearly as Cara could determine his name) turning now and again to relay information to his folk. Before midday the warning was given, and the People brought forth food from their burrows in the rock walls and gestured for their guests to eat. No stranger meal could any mortal ever have eaten, it seemed to Cara, as she munched a sort of bread that seemed made from lichen and pollen and sipped pale green wine whose origin, she surmised, must have lain with mosses and maidenhair ferns.

Their meal made, they touched hand to forehead, in the sign of thanks to their hosts, and took their leave. Not by the hard ways in which they had come did they go, for now they sought him whom they had avoided. Down the smooth slopes from the heights they made their way, using the paths of the People. The bare bones of the mountain they left behind and descended into rock-studded meadows where, in summer, the horned ones of the forest grazed. Now the grasslands were bare of life and of green, and the two women moved across them quietly, stepping with the flowing gait of the hunter who fears to start his prey too soon.

"He moves upon the heights," said Tisha, as they paused to feel the space about them. "His camp lies below us, in a hollow rimmed with stones and juniper, so Wheesha told me. But now he seeks for strange game and never thinks himself hunted."

"Do we lie in wait above his camping-place?" asked Cara.

"Such is my thought," smiled her mother.

So, long before sunset, they lay snugly burrowed into a ridge of junipers, on the lip of the cup which held the hunter's gear. Sleeping and watching by turns, they waited with the patience they had learned as a part of their lives and their beings, seldom stirring so much as a foot or a finger, breathing so softly that they could not hear one another.

The sun went down behind the gray mass of cloud which had hidden it all the day, and with the coming darkness the man came seeking his fire and his food and his bed. Tisha felt him first and laid her hand lightly upon Cara's wrist. Then the girl strained her senses and caught the bundle of sensations that was the man, walking dispiritedly among the stones of the mountainside.

Never had Cara been so near to another of humankind, save only her mother. She lay tense with astonishment at the intricate orchestration of mood and emotion that existed within him. His thoughts were impenetrable to the delicate talent which was hers and her mother's, but his feelings closed above her as a stream over the head of an inexperienced swimmer, and she sought desperately to disengage herself from them. Then she felt Tisha's cool fingers again on her wrist, then her temple, and the tide drained away, leaving her limp.

A bud of fire kindled below, which soon blossomed into a grateful glow. The scent of cooking found its way upward to the place where Tisha and Cara lay, but they kept their motionless watch. Once, far and woeful, came the cry of the People, and the man in the hollow raised his head to listen, as if seeking to fix the direction from which the sound came. No motion, no sensation concerning him was lost upon the watchers on the rim of the hollow. Their eyes never left his figure, their ears were attuned to the sounds he made, and their sensing probed, unfelt, into the deeps of his heart.

When he had eaten, he took into his lap the weapon he loved best and began again to hone the blade. Then did Tisha rise, to stand upon the edge of the rim, her figure lit against the dark sky by the red firelight. Followed by Cara, she leaped lightly down into the cup of rock, and they stood silent, facing the startled man, who had sprung erect, holding his spear at the ready. Then, seeing them to be women, he laughed and laid aside the spear.

"Little did I think to have loveliness beside my fire this night," he said and swept a playful bow.

"We are not come as guests," answered Tisha, her cool voice falling clearly into the little space. "We waited while you rested and warmed yourself and ate; we allowed you to have your weapon at hand. We have hunted you as prey for two days, and now we have you at our hands. You have come into the world we have chosen as ours, and you are bearing death in your heart for all not as yourself. We are come to do battle for the Wildings and the People of the Heights, and for all the little beasts without the power of speech. We have slain the hart when the snow lay heavy and hunger stood at our door. We have snared the rabbit and the wildfowl when we needed food. But never have we sought the death of another with the clear flame of joy which burns in your heart."

"You think to stay me from my hunting?" he asked. He laughed again, "Overmountain, I have slain all manner of beasts until I have grown weary of the smell of their blood. Here in this wilderness I see tracks I do not know, and in the forest I almost slew a beast which walked like a man and looked at me with golden eyes that knew what I did. No man, even, could prevent my walking abroad, spear in hand, to slay what I wish. You are welcome to share my fire, but speak no more of battle with me. I am Heraad, and none has ever overcome me."

"Until now," said Cara. Then she, with her mother, bent her will upon the man. He grasped his spear and sought to lift it, but their combined wills forced his hand to open, and the haft slid away. As a child bends a reed, so they moved him to sit, flattened against the stone where he was wont to lie.

"We are going to show you what life is," said Tisha. "Come with us, that you may learn and live; for if you do not, you will die."

Then she joined hands with her daughter, and their spirits seized that part of Heraad which was capable of

feeling and of learning and bore it away with their seeking senses into the heights above.

Among the burrows of the People they went, less per-
ceptible than the air, seeing the folk of the high places
about their evening's pastimes and tasks. Young ones
rolled in firelight within the stony caves, and their
mothers scolded them in their strange-sounding tongue,
when they were overly noisy and interfered with the
doings of the elders. Groups of males sat about fires, play-
ing at toss-bones or talking earnestly. The females were
about their supper-making or clearing-away which,
though far different in detail from the ways of men, yet
were so obviously what they were that the differences
were as nothing. One nursed a youngling with an injured
foot, murmuring in its furry ear and soothing its tears
away. One, in a lonely burrow, sat in darkness, head in
hands, alone with some private grief. Two sat snuggled
into a secluded corner, fingers twined together, whispering tenderly.

Then, in a swift whirl and blur of motion, they swept
their captive down from the heights into the flowing forest lands of the valley. Deep into the dells where the
Wildings dwelt, they moved, seeking here and there until
they found a snug place, roofed with an ancient moon-
tree that leaned protectively over the Wilding-lair. There,
too, burned a fire in a rock-built hearth and in its flickering they could see the woven vines and broad plaited
grasses that made the walls, the deep beds of bracken, the
settles cut from gnarled stumps and leggy branches. And
there Wildings were sitting, dreaming into the fire, holding each a young one. All seemed drowsy and at peace,

looking with golden eyes into golden flame, and as they watched one of the little ones dropped into sleep and its head drooped gently into the curve of its father's arm. No walls of stone had ever held what was more truly a family.

Then they came, more slowly than they went, back across the forest and the hills to the place where their bodies sat, stopping, now and again, to peer into a little burrow where one of the small beasts slept or watched.

Gently as the leaves of the moon-tree falling, they settled back into themselves, at last, but still they held Heraad captive to their wills. Now they moved close to him and sat before him, and Tisha looked into his eyes.

"These are the people whom you would hunt," she said. "One of their number you have wounded sorely, and many of them might you slay, given the freedom to carry death. They are not as you and I upon the surfaces of their skins; but within they think, they feel, they suffer and they rejoice. Even the little beasts have within them the gift of life, if not of thought, and this you would wrest from them in sport. Not for this did the gods give you life and strength."

Then they eased their grip upon the man, and he slumped against the rock. His eyes held awe and terror. "What manner of women are you, that you may hold me without hands and compel me without weapons?" he gasped. "In my own place, you might rule as goddesses, possessed of such powers. What need have you of these cattle you have shown me? They are none of yours, for they walk free and do not serve you. Return with me to the world overmountain, and we three shall hold all there is within our grasp."

Cara's lip curled as she answered, "Know you not, ignorant man, that those who walk in the ways of the gods, valuing all their gifts and keeping all their laws, are sometimes given strange potencies, but that, should they use them ill, those gifts can be swiftly withdrawn—even the greatest of them, which is life? This I learned in the cradle, and much I wonder at those who had your teaching as their duty. Did they teach you nothing of what is real? Did they never hold bread to your tongue and say, "This is the fruit of sun and soil and the sweat of men. Savor it, for it is precious'? Did they never take you into the forest that you might learn the ways of the small folk who balance upon the wheel of life? Did they never say to you, 'Live, my child, in the light of truth and reason, that you may stand before the gods as one of their own, when you come to the door that opens into otherwhere'?"

But Heraad stared at her as though she spoke in a strange tongue. "My folk are wise and thrifty and are noble and wealthy. Why should they fill my small head with that which will put no gold in my pouch and no game in my bag? We laugh when we find humor, we weep when we suffer, and we kill when the mood is in us. What else can life hold?" And his dark eyes were puzzled, seeking for their purpose, without comprehension.

Then Cara turned to her mother and said, "Truly you told me. There is no light in the 'world,' only darkness of self-seeking." She turned aside her face into the shadow, for tears were in her eyes.

"These are the laws of life which we teach you, Heraad," said Tisha sternly. "You must learn either to value lives other than your own or to fear—greatly to fear

—this place where you now draw breath. Not otherwise may you go from here as a living man. We do not take your life lightly, and for this reason only do you stand this side of the door of death. As we compel you to sit, so can we do other things. We can stop your heart from its long duty. We can erase the tiny streams that bear your thought from brain to limb. We can, without stirring, send you forth to face the gods in their own place, leaving this shell of you for the fowl of the air and the small beasts to worry, at leisure, as you would have worried them, given the opportunity. Fear us, Heraad, for we are not as you. We are more alien than the Wilding in the dell or the People of the Heights. We see through other eyes than yours into places that are not to be seen by your kind. And we are stronger than you. Not only in our spirits, but in our bodies might we overcome you. Forget your women of the towns when you look upon us. We survive in the wilds, without heeding danger or discomfort. We set hand to tree and to stone and to labors you have never done. Fear us, Heraad!"

Then she sat still, looking into his eyes with all the strength of her spirit moving between them. Heraad seemed to shrink against the stone, and his knuckles whitened upon his taut hands. Cara moved beside her mother and took her hand, closed her eyes, and sent her strength through the clasp. For long they sat thus, as the fire went to scattered embers and the night curved toward dawn.

Into the dark hollow that was the mind of the man they poured all that they knew of true feeling . . . love in a golden river, compassion enough to burst the heart, joy that lit the mind with starbursts of glory. And they also poured fear, terror, sorrow, grief, all the passions that grind the lives of men between their stones. They filled Heraad as though he were an empty cup, cracking the dry walls of his ignorant conceit and crumbling the foundations of his youthful arrogance.

The light of the new day found them all asleep, dropped where they sat in utter weariness. The clouds had departed in the night, and frost hung upon the junipers in the newly minted sunlight. The first rays awakened Heraad, who stirred uneasily, then sat erect in alarm.

Those whom he feared lay sleeping before him. His hand went to his spear, and he rose and bent over the two who had so wrenched his life from its pattern. In the clear light, their faces were marked with beauty and peace and purity and weariness. No sign was there of the terrible strengths they possessed; they were defenseless now. He lifted his spear and straightened, bringing his arm back as if to strike. But, in the midst of the motion, he looked into the sky and about the little hollow of rock, as though he were bewildered.

Upon a juniper, just above his head, sat a Grack, its head cocked to one side, staring at him with curious black eyes. He looked into those knowing eyes and, for a heartbeat, he felt the swift throb of the blood through its body, the chill of the juniper twig in its claws, the light gnawing of morning hunger in its belly.

Slowly he lowered the spear. Moving quietly, he put his scattered belongings into his pack and fastened it onto his shoulders. He lifted the spear again and studied it as though it were some strange artifact found by accident.

Then he thrust it deep into the earth beside the sleeping women and turned toward the mountains, moving away into the eye of the sun.

Before the Grack had flown away, Tisha woke. The shadow of the spear lay across her face, and she turned and touched Cara. Together they sat in the abandoned hollow, feeling the dwindling presence that was Heraad move away, into his own place, leaving their world to its lawful tenants.

Part II:

The Shuttles Move

Narrative of Shanah ni Raithe do Raithe

Fallowden of the Raithes had stood from time past any remembering. Its lichened stones rise from the rolling lands about, marking its boundaries with walls and standing against the wind to form the cross-shaped hall. The flags of its garden have rung to the armored heel of the conqueror more than once, and the beams of the speaking-chamber have held the hanged bodies of more than one of its masters.

For the Raithes of Fallowden are not malleable folk, and the arm of might, if threatened, must fall. Long has the house stood abandoned, while those who held it in heart lay hidden in the distant mountains and forests. Yet always have we returned to our own, though months and years may have passed while it held counsel with none but winds and waters. The old hall has held our lives and our pride for generations untold, and in our absence it has sheltered other fugitives from the wild times and the hard hands of overlords.

Always, always, we have returned. From across the Purple Waters, from the mountains, we have come again to Fallowden, and it has received us into its strong and stony self as though we had never left it. Being no family for hoarding rich furnishings and things of value, we have found it always much as we left it, with its rude comfort unharmed by those other souls whom we would have welcomed there, had we been at home.

Alone it stands in the rolling leagues of pasture land, neighbored by none save the beasts and the fowl of the air. None has ever stood beside us when we defied the powers of the world; no others have ever found the hardihood to live in the lonely lands about, for all their fertile grace. For in the wildlands, Those Who Wait walk on the wind, and their words penetrate wood and stone and chill him who basks before the fire and her who walks upon the stair. Yet they harm none, and we have pitied them often and sought to learn what might give them solace.

There were nine of us there, in my time. The Raithe himself still lived, tenth great-grandson of him who built the hall, and a hale man he was and full of vigor, for all his ninety years. His daughter Talitha was his right hand, for she possessed the gift of long sight, which we of the family are wont to have, and he relied upon her reports of doings afar and in the future.

Then there were the three sons of my parents, long dead. Born with the hunter's mark, they were seldom at table, and almost never within the chamber when the fires burned high for talk. Only by the game we ate did we know they still made their home with us. Ruthella, my sister, was minded to tend the management of the house, and well-pleased were we to honor her whim, while her bright-haired husband, Millis, brought laughter and good cheer to us all, as he went about bringing the ancient orchard to fruition again, and drew our neglected garden from its weedy depression into full-bodied good humor.

Raf, my man, was also a Raithe, though of a cousinly

branch, so that I, the youngest, wildest, most carefree—
and spoilt—of the lot had but added to our number by my
marriage. We both had the dark and savage air of the
Raithes and those few outlanders we met took us for sib-
lings. And so we were, in spirit, for we loved the wild
winds that swept the lands about, and we moved as one
with the herds of horses, which were our family's means
of livelihood and our own particular task. Ardently we
loved and bitterly fought and warmly made up again, so
that life was full of excitement and interest.

In the evenings, especially in winter when the voices
called madly across the gale, we would sit between the
fires which burned at the ends of the chamber, singing,
sometimes, or telling tales of our longfathers, or laughing
at Millis's wit, yet feeling inside our bones the chill of
loneliness which the waiting ones cried of. Then would I
sometimes look up into the shadows of the beams and
fancy I could see other shadows, swinging gently in an
unfelt breeze, and I would feel the presence of the long
and unbroken line of Raithe, focused in the chamber, at
one with us all.

But that was a winter when I was much given to fan-
cies, for I carried our child. Bitter was my grief that I
could not go out into the icy gales with Raf to tend the
horses, and so would I have done, but he spoke to me
of our debt to the past and the future and so gentled
me to the bit of my present condition. Yet I was restless
without my usual work, and often I would help Ruthella
about the house. But most often I would seek out my
grandsir, where he sat before the grate in his room at
the head of the stair, and ask him for tales of our folk,
from their beginnings.

Yet the Raithe seemed abstracted. His papers lay before him untouched by the quill, and his studbooks lay unopened. He roused himself from his deep thought when I was by and rolled upon his tongue the old tales for my enjoyment, but I could see that he was troubled, and at last I asked him for the cause. Talitha, who sat by, mending and dreaming, started, and my grandsir looked at me keenly, as if considering.

"It is best that you know what we dread, for you have more to lose—or to save—than any of your kin," he said at last. "Talitha," and he turned to her, "Tell the child what you have seen, that she may begin to take thought."

My aunt's hand was steady, and her needle picked evenly in and out of the heavy cloak upon her lap, yet I could see a quiver of despair beneath its very steadfastness. "It is not certain—I can never be quite certain—remember this, Shanah. Yet I have seen, as I went about my work, or tended Father, or dropped into sleep of a night, strange boots striding our hall and blood once more upon the flags of the chamber. I have looked afar, with my inner seeing, toward the City of Lirith. There I see a new ruler, mad with a rage for power, and a new order of things which may not rest until all that has been is overset. I see a new exile, child, and new deaths, and new voices among Those Who Wait."

She fell silent, sewing, with her eyes upon the cloth.

Then the Raithe spoke. "Never has my daughter erred in such a seeing. We sit between these beloved walls, feeling the goodness which has for so long been ours, learning—or seeking to learn—to lose all that we have and are, and might yet be." He sighed and looked into the fire, and I sat, chilled with foreboding, waiting for him to speak again.

"You have a good man, child, and lack of courage has never been among your faults. You are a survivor—aye, for I've seen a few of the kind in my life. You can live, with your child, and carry forward the name of Raithe, to bide in some fastness until the signs change again, and it is safe to return to Fallowden. Draw near me—I must tell you something strange and rather fearsome, and I would take your hand in mine."

I went and knelt beside him before the fire, and held his hand. He smiled down at me, and his black eyes were unfaded and proud as he said, "Only in time of peril do we burden our younglings with this old and bitter secret. Yet there is in this strange thing aid for all of the house of Raithe. For Those Who Wait, whom you hear on the wind and feel in the chill of your bones, those waiting ones are . . . were . . . of our blood. They are those of our house who fell in wrath upon this land, in this house, defending their own from those rapacious ones who ever seem to be spawning in the outworld . . ." He paused at my gasp of comprehension. "And they are kindly disposed toward us, who are their distant children. One who flees for life across the wildlands may find guidance in their cries. Your grandam and I were the last to follow them to safety. We had hoped to be the last ever to take that dark road. But, should you be driven forth, follow them if they call to you. Follow them . . . follow them . . ." And he seemed to drift again into his dark dream.

Talitha rose and took my hand, leading me from the chamber. In her room, she turned and motioned me to sit.

"You are pale, Shanah. Let me find cordial," and she rummaged in her cabinet and drew forth a bottle of rosy liquid which she handed me. It was warm in the throat and the blood, and my heart resumed its pace.

"Did you see . . . oh, Talitha, whose deaths did you see?" I cried at last, dreading her answer.

"Death there was, but none to name," she answered. "I would not look, and would not tell had I done. None needs to feel that terrible loss until its reality is upon him. And remember, child, this may be only an old woman's dream. Take thought, prepare, but do not despair before that which may not come to be."

Then we sat, silent, sipping the cordial, which sent its transient glow through our veins but could not warm our coldly foreboding hearts.

When we gathered in the beamed kitchen for our evening meal, all seemed warmth and light and good smells of food, so that I felt that the happening of the afternoon must have been some weird daydream. But when I looked at my grandsir, I knew that it had not; still he had the look of one who has not quite waked from nightmare. Raf noticed also, and whispered to me that the old man seemed unwell. I nodded and pressed his hand, but could not yet speak with him of the thing which now darkened my thoughts.

But when all were settled before the fires in the speaking-chamber, then the Raithe stood upon his stone hearth and turned toward us, and all fell silent, feeling his words before they were uttered.

"My children," he began, "we have lived in good fortune for long in this, our home. It may be . . . it may be that we are coming to an end, now, of the days of ease and comfort." Then, standing, tall and dark against the red flames, he told of Talitha's visions.

When he fell silent, we sat for a time without words, without questions. Raf took my hand in his and leaned his cheek against mine, and I knew that he understood my strangeness earlier. The firelight leaped and danced about the chamber, lighting our faces with a warmth we could not feel. Again I seemed to see the old shadows swaying among the beams, and the voices that came on the wind now spoke to me in a tongue I seemed to understand.

For once, our three brothers were with us. Eris, Irian, and Perrin sat in their usual dark silence, but their eyes were like embers banked in a nightfire, and I almost pitied any outlanders who met them in their wrath. When Eris stood to speak, we turned our faces to him in surprise; seldom was he, or any of them, heard to speak save to one another.

"We are Raithes," he said. "All are able, in our own ways, and all are strong with our own strengths. Our paths have lain in the wildlands and the forests of the far hills, so these we know as we know our fingers. Fear not, if all comes to worst, to flee into the rough places. Even in winter, there is shelter in the pine forests, game to be found, roots and bark that will sustain life. We will fight, as have our fathers in many lost years. We will lose, for nine cannot stand against troops of warriors, however fiercely we give battle. Some may survive. To them we say, 'Go north, into the mountains. There is a hope of safety, and there they will not pursue you for long, for they fear to go among Those Who Wait.'" He stood for a moment looking from one to another of us speculatively. Then he nodded abruptly and sat.

The Raithe nodded too and said, "Well spoken, grandson, and truly. I can give no better advice." And then he told them of Those Who Wait, and I saw eyes light with understanding and heads lift and turn to catch the wails that moaned faintly in the night. As had mine, their eyes turned upward to the firelit beams, and we all saw, within our spirits, the shapes of hanged men swaying there. But they were no shapes of fear, nor had they ever been. Those of our blood had died defending Fallowden, and their wan presences were Raithe, as were we.

Ruthella, ever practical, crossed to the hearth beside our grandsir and said, "We shall prepare packs of supplies, light to carry but filled with dried fruits and meats and wrapped in blankets. They shall ever be refreshed, when needful and shall lie ready to hand should a need for them arise. None need go out into the inhospitable lands empty-handed." And she and her Millis went from the chamber and we could hear their steps tapping along the flagged passage to the storerooms.

Then we looked at one another with love and regret and went about our own tasks, the brothers moving silently away in single file, as though upon a hunt in their beloved forests. Raf and I lingered a moment with the Raithe and Talitha.

"We shall drive the horses afar into the pasturelands and the eastern hills," Raf said. "There they shall thrive and multiply, unbeknownst to those who come, for it is in my mind that the horses of Fallowden have ever been the magnet that drew the oppressors to our door. If they are not to be found, though we perish one and all, we have won a little victory."

My grandsir smiled. "Aye, drive them out. The stud-books shall be hidden below in the dry well, with all records and notations. To those who come, there shall be no smell of horses about our holding. But those who are driven out, if any there be, will know; and those who return, if ever any may, will again have a way of livelihood at hand."

Then we went to our chamber and donned warm clothing and fur-lined boots and went out into the paddock to saddle our mounts. No word was said of my condition, for well we knew that the child and I must harden ourselves to worse hardship than this, should that which was foreseen come to pass.

So we went out into the night, amid the cries of our ancient fathers, and roused the horses from their sheltered dreams of summer grass, driving them from the hayricks and hedges into the full bite of the wind. The flame in the lightglass glinted in their puzzled eyes as we turned them from their home and chivied them into the wild, and our hearts were wrenched, for they were like our children and we loved them.

Morning found us far to the east, among the hills and gullies that edged the forested ridges. Then we rested and warmed ourselves and ate, and our charges stood about us, shivering and snorting and stamping in the cold. But short was our respite, and soon we moved again eastward, around the shoulders of the great ridges which sheltered the far valleys from the worst of the wind and the snow. Great was our relief when we found these meadows only scantily snow-laden, with generous thatches of dry grasses and many sheltering pine thickets for the comfort of the herd. They were tough beasts, and we had never coddled them; but always there had been hay and protection from the winds, and these we sought to provide in this distant place.

We urged them into the thickets upon the slopes, scattering them well, and then we rode on into the east, making a wide circuit, that they might not seek to follow us. Well we knew that they could find their way home, but with the storm which now blew, we felt that they would remain in the sheltered valleys. So we turned our backs upon our herd. If tears of grief froze upon our faces, they were lost among the tears of cold, and neither of us spoke of it.

Now we rode into the teeth of the storm, and pellets of sleet mixed with the snow to form a bitter pall. Our horses wearied, but we could not let them rest, or all of us would freeze, so we drove them back into the west for as long as they could manage. Then we sheltered in the lee of a hill and made a fire. The horses drew as near as they could to the small blaze, and we measured grain from our saddle-packs into their nosebags. Fuel was scanty, but we ranged outward, gathering twigs and brush and twists of dried grass to feed our flame. So we bought a few hours' rest, but too soon it was time to face the gale again.

The cold and the long hours in the saddle were making themselves felt—both to me and to the child. At first he had moved, as if disturbed at the motions of riding. Then, as I tired, he quieted, which aided my breathing. But when we remounted to finish our journey, he again squirmed sharply, causing me to gasp as I seated myself in the saddle. Raf moved near and leaned to touch my cheek.

"Is all well, Shanah? This has been a bitter task. May the gods grant it has not harmed you or the youngling."

I turned my face to lay my cheek against his glove. "We are well, love, but not quite happy with the present state of things. Let us but reach home again, however short the span we may remain there, and I shall be grateful."

Dark came early—truly, the light of day had not really pierced the sky all the day. We rode on, seeing by snow-light, saving the lightglass. And when the lights of Fallowden at last glimmered through the flying snow, we felt great relief.

Millis waited in the stables to take our horses. "We expected you. Talitha saw you coming long ere you came into view. Warm food and your heated bed wait. Go you to your ease, and I shall make your mounts comfortable and turn them into their stalls."

Then we turned gratefully to the house and rest, shutting out the cold wastes behind us and forgetting, for the brief space of sleep, the threat which kept us company.

Truly our winter's peace was broken. Yet the trouble in our hearts was soothed, somewhat, by the labors which we now took up, as all was made ready for siege and battle and flight—or death. We turned out the armory and brought the weapons it held into the light of day, sharpening, polishing, cleaning, making all useful again.

Long had it been since our halls and stair had held lances and swords in the iron racks upon their walls.

Arrows bristled from the baskets where Ruthella had arranged dried grasses, and when we sat in the chamber in the evening, all whetted heads and fletched more arrows, for we knew that spring would bring any trouble that came, and by then I would be in no condition for combat.

My station was the stairhead, and certain hours of the day were set aside when none walked through the area below, as I improved my skill at placing the long shafts in every part of the lower hall and the doorways leading into it. I pulled a heavy bow, and the thick scraps of wood which were my targets often bristled with arrows which had been driven cleanly through them.

Much thought had been given to my escape, for all were in agreement that I must survive, with the child, that there might be a future for the house of Raithe. This the Raithe ended simply, for he delved into his oldest memories and recalled a hidden stair which led to a passage cut into the thickness of the wall. This, in turn, linked with a passage in the garden wall which abutted the house at a corner. Following the hollow walls, it meandered for almost a half-league before coming out at a door hidden in a wall which faced toward the northern pastures. There Raf made a lightly fenced paddock and kept Gollas, my gelding, and his heavy-haunched Plana, that there might be a means of flight, should any make it so far.

The packs of supplies we distributed in entryways and outbuildings, as well as within the invisible tunnel. Thus, however one might find it necessary to flee, he would readily find a parcel that might sustain him in the wild.

In other years, the turning of the season had brought joy to our hearts, and this, we had felt, should be even more joyful than any other, bringing, as it did, the hope of our child. But the melting of the snows signaled the beginning of our travails, and we saw the fruit trees budding with a sense of final disaster heavy upon us.

Now my breath grew short and my temper shorter. My fiery Raf, no patient man by nature, found it necessary to labor outdoors for most of the day, principally to escape my tongue. And, truly, I was ashamed of myself, but so heavy and weary had I become that everything and everyone rasped on my raw nerve unbearably. The greening of the spring was a pain in my spirit, and I lay awake many nights, breathing carefully and quietly, dreading that which must come and bargaining with the gods for the life of my child. Often, when I lay with hot and silent tears behind my eyes, Raf would turn and touch my shoulder gently; and I would know that his sleep was the counterfeit equal of mine, and that he, too, was wrestling with the future.

With the snow's disappearance, my three brothers went abroad to keep watch upon the southern ways. Each came to me in my chamber and stood beside my chair, where I spent much time, now, making the padding and carrying-bags I would need in order to help the child to survive. So alike were they as they stood there with their concern plain upon their dark faces that I found it possible to smile and to say to them all, "Go with the gods, my brothers. Well am I in mind and body. Go you to your chosen tasks and know that I shall accomplish mine, if the gods will that I live."

Their awkward hugs, spiced with beardy scratches, almost brought tears, but I smiled again and said, "What we must, that will we all do. Love goes with you, and hope and concern."

But their going was a dark thing, and I knew that I might never see their dear faces again. And all that day, Raf found tasks near at hand, that I might know the comfort of his presence. Now I found myself strangely at peace, at grips with the coming days. No sharp word passed my lips thenceforward, for which my husband must have been grateful.

As the weeks passed, we grew taut and fine-drawn. Our ears seemed attuned to catch strange footsteps, and our eyes strayed southward too often. The cloud of apple blossom in the orchard was no comfort to our hearts, nor the lilac before the door. The time drew near when my child should come to birth, and I knew with every thread of my spirit that war and death would come upon us before my child drew first breath. Talitha would not confirm my presentiment, but she did not deny it. And a night came when she stood beside the Raithe before the hearth and said, "They come. Our hunters come over the pasturelands, and our enemies come upon the road. The time is at hand. Before tomorrow is gone to darkness, our fates will be read into the book of time."

Then the Raithe raised his hands in the old gesture and turned his eyes upward to the shadows among the beams. "War is again upon us. You, who are our longfathers, have traveled the road before us, even to its most bitter ending, and your shades have bided among us through all the good years. Now, with the aid of the gods, guide our feet, strengthen our arms, make deadly our aim, and, for the continuance of our name, help forth any of us who may survive this coming day."

Though no wind blew, we heard in faint chorus the voices of Those Who Wait, wailing upon the lands about, and a new note of anguish filled them. The old shadows moved among the beams, and we were strangely comforted. Even should we fall here, as did they, we knew that there would be a continuance.

Then there were footsteps upon the flags of the porch, and Ruthella hastened to open the heavy oaken door, that our brothers might enter. They filed in, dark and silent as ever, and with them came a cold purpose that settled into the fibers of us all, as we greeted them.

"They are encamped just to the south," said Irian. "Most like, they had intended to take us in darkness, but Those Who Wait dogged them with wailings as they came, and when night fell they could no longer control their horses—nor themselves, I'd wager. The morning will see them at our door. They will not move until dawn, wherefore all should rest as best we may, that we may take many with us into the land of death."

Our grandsir laid his hands upon them, one by one, as if in blessing. "You are our outward bulwark," he said. "Rest you now, and tomorrow we shall walk in pride to our destinies, as Raithes have always walked."

So we went to our beds, Raf and I to love fiercely and then to sleep in utter dreamlessness. But when first light crept between the hangings, we woke completely and turned to cling one last time, lip to lip, before rising to meet this most dreadful of days.

When the sun rose, it found an armed camp where the peace of Fallowden had reigned for so long. My brothers were concealed in hedges along the road, armed with bows, and planning to give our visitors their first greeting from the house of Raithe. Millis and Raf hid where they commanded view of the rear and principal doors. The Raithe waited in the speaking-chamber, armed in mail and carrying his great mace.

Talitha stood beside him, booted and breeched, with her sword at hand and a basket of light lances at her back, while Ruthella, garbed likewise, held the entryway. I was at my place upon the stairhead, but only a loose robe would fit me now, and I was denied the freedom of movement which the others knew. Nonetheless, I was well-armed and helmed with good steel, that no chance blow or arrow might shake my wits. All was in readiness, and we armed our spirits with patience, for well we knew the prechewed terrors of waiting.

The sun marked its old arc toward noon, and there was no untoward movement upon the road, no strange sound to drown the voice of the graybird which sang its mating song upon the lilac. I sat on cushions against the railing, watching the thin arc of road which was visible through the one high window in my line of vision. Now and again the three below exchanged low-pitched comments, and once or twice Raf entered the house to see how I fared, but we all waited tranquilly, without tension—almost with joy—for the coming battle. For it was thinkable that, granted long lives of peace and ease, we might have become soft, malleable, townlike folk, losing the strength that was the blood of Raithe, the honor that sustained our house in pride and invincible courage. For all our lives, we had been trained for this trial, hardened against this struggle, and we could not grieve that the time had come to test our mettle.

Long before the sun drew overhead, we heard, far to the south, a clamor of cries and the neighing of horses. Then the Raithe shouted, "The huntsmen of Raithe have found their prey! They chivy the enemy upon either hand, driving them with arrows flown from no visible hand."

Talitha was chanting now, and her words made a rhythm below his cry. "Now the forces of outland waver, seeking upon the right and the left for their attackers. Still they come, leaving a thin line of their dead in the dust of the road, but our huntsmen come more swiftly, all three, untouched by the hand of the enemy.

"Upon the road there is blood, and horses run, unreined and masterless. The captains cry out and threaten; the lines are re-forming. But our kinsmen are upon the wall . . . now they pass the orchard . . . and now they are at the door."

Then, surely, their steps rang upon the flagstones, and the shapes of my brothers flitted darkly across the light that framed the door. I heard their voices joined with those of the others, and quickly they came to the foot of the stair and looked up at me.

"Our sister, you carry the future of our race within you. Peril comes quickly, and we must go to our places; but we implore you, do not wait too long to flee your post. Seek the hidden door before any draw near enough to see it close behind you. We have saddled the horses and bound your necessary supplies upon them, that you may go with all haste. With the help of the gods, we shall see that your man goes with you; but even should you go alone, go with speed. Our love and pride ride with you." So spoke Perrin, and all three raised their hands in the old gesture. I raised my visor and kissed my hand to them, but I could not speak.

Now the approaching horses could be felt in the throbbing vibration of hooves. No horn blew, no voice shouted, but that rising thunder traced the course of our enemies as they drew near. I closed my helm with a clang, and my grandsir cried from the chamber, "The gods be with my children!"

The time of battle was upon us.

A voice called a command, and the hoof-noise ceased, leaving a strange quiet. Ruthella, peering through the slit in the barred door, called softly, "Our brothers are in the orchard, arrows nocked. Now!"

And the twang of bowstrings pierced the silence, and cries rose again from those upon the road. I tried frantically to see through the slit-window, but its angle was too high, and I could only listen, as the sounds of shouts and cries and moans and the clang of sword-blades filled the space before our door. I saw the graybird fly past the window, dismayed at the carnage about his nest. Then I heard a terrific blow against the door, and the heavy beam groaned.

"Back, Ruthella," cried the Raithe. "Leave them the entryway, and chivy them from the doorway. If you are there, they may crush you when they break through."

Then Ruthella came into my view, as she slipped aside to shelter behind the doorframe, sword in hand, and her basket of lances behind her. Not too soon did she move, for with another grinding crack the door gave, and my sister thrust with her sword and drew it back brighter than it went and dripping with blood.

"Ni Raithe! Ni Raithe!" she cried, and her shout was echoed within the house and without, and I heard the voice of Raf among the noise. Then I drew my bow, and Talitha and my grandsir came to stand behind my sister.

With shouting and stamping, men burst into the hall below and fell before the swords and the mace of the three who awaited them. I found a tall helm clear of the press and aimed at the joint between helm and corselet. The string sang by my cheek, and the arrow sank from view along with the tall figure it felled. Then I turned my attention to any who stood clear of my folk, and I felled them as I had pierced the blocks of wood, one arrow to one target.

The hall was now a dreadful moil of blood and stench and noise. I could not see Ruthella, when I spared a glance, but my grandsir's mace swung high and fell, swung high and fell, steadily as time. Now three men sprang for the stair, intending to put an end to my deadly hail of arrows. Two I slew in the hall and the third upon the second step, for I had no wish to fly so soon from the battle of my people.

As I aimed again into the crowded hall, I saw Talitha fall, pierced by a sword. Her slayer fell upon her, my arrow through his neck. Then there came a stir among those in the entryway, and a voice of authority shouted, "Rush the stair. Those two will keep, for the time. Get that archer at the stairhead!"

Then I knew that it was time for me to depart, leaving those whom I loved to die, and I half-rose, shooting over the railing, and slew the owner of that voice as he emerged into the hall. Then I turned and hurried into the passageway where my door was hidden. As it whispered shut behind me, I heard the clank of spurs and the jangle of mail and weapons at the head of the passage, but I had safely gone to earth, with my precious burden which, perhaps, was all that was left of the house of Raithe.

Voices filled the hall, and I laughed to myself, amid all the dread and grief, at their puzzled exclamations.

"She went this way—I saw her clearly. A woman, and with child, or I'm no father."

"One with the power of invisibility, no doubt," commented another, sarcastically.

"Or one with a secret bolthole!" said a third. "Tap the walls—we may yet find our elusive bowlady."

My breath had now steadied a little, and I set myself to draw across the door the thick panel, which had been provided for just such a case. When it was in place, I knew that I had breathing space, for, even should they strip the wooden walls away, the panel would seem just as that understructure which lined all of the passage. No tap upon my hidden door would sound differently from a tap upon the solid panels beside it.

Now I fumbled in the darkness for the lightglass which had been set ready for me, and the white glimmer of its kindling comforted my bruised heart. Awkwardly, taking my time, I traversed the narrow ways, moved heavily down cobwebby stairs, and found myself in the earth-floored tunnels which lined the garden walls. I stopped for a moment to ease my racing pulse, and as I stood, breathing deeply, I felt within myself a sudden difference, faint and distant, as if some silent alarm had been rung, or a wordless warning given. The child had been quiet for long, but a quiver could be felt deep within, and I knew that this day would see the birth of Raf's youngling.

So I hurried, indeed, along that dark and angled way toward my gate into the wilds. Many stops for rest slowed me, yet I made fair speed, and before midafternoon I looked out upon our pastureland and the horses, saddled and laden with packs, that awaited me.

Gollas, grazing at the end of the paddock, raised his head and nickered at my call, then came at the gallop, followed by Plana. I was weeping as I tightened their girths and fitted on their bitless bridles, for I heard in my heart Raf's voice saying, "If none goes with you, leave no horse behind. If any survive, we shall make escape as best we may, but no horse of ours must fall into the hands of yon merciless men. They would place bits in the tender mouths and rowel the sleek sides with spurs, which no beast of ours has ever known. Leave none of our hooved children to their enslavement!"

I rode away from Fallowden with the sun slanting across my way, touching the young grass with amber, and all the tender scents and sounds of spring wrapping me round. But the black anger within my spirit colored all, and only the faint calls of Those Who Wait spoke to my inner self. Yet the voices were not angry, only infinitely sad, as I moved toward them, among them. I believe that I saw them, moving like cloud-shadows across the grass-lands, though no cloud stained the sky. And the calls led me on, always northward.

Now riding became very hard, for the muscles that held the child in place knotted and squeezed, seized me in spasms and released me. I clung to Gollas, unable to guide with heel and rein, as he was accustomed. But he also followed the calls, for he was Raithe-bred for generations and used to obeying Raithes, visible or no. At last, I knew that we must halt, for the breath-stopping spasms had changed, becoming long up-and-down movements, irresistible as season-change or sunrise.

I dropped from the saddle to land upon legs that would not hold me. Clinging to the straps, I hastily untied the bag of necessities which Talitha had prepared for me, instructing me in the uses of all. Then I sank into a crouch, as she had taught me, and gave myself over to the rhythms of the earth and the sea and the movements of the planets in the heavens. The circle of voices closed in, as if trying to comfort me, but there was no comfort in that world of colossal labors.

There came an end at last, and I drew from beneath my billowing robe a redly furious man-child, who needed no slap to spur him into his first cry. I tended him and wiped him dry and laid him in the carry-bag which I had made, then returned to more efforts. When all was done, and I had cleaned myself and made certain that none might trace me by signs upon the earth, I tried to mount Gollas, but there was no strength left within me, and I could not.

There was a soft call behind me, and I turned, with the child in my arm, and went blindly, using will to move me. I found myself beneath a pine tree, stunted but hardy, that had laid a smooth carpet of needles beneath branches that swept to touch the earth on three sides. Then I sank down into sleep that was dreamless as death.

Narrative of Lengalyon the Hermit

Oftentimes, upon this wind-buffeted crag, I am minded of the gray eagle that quartered the skies of my youth. Many a dream he unwittingly bore upon his weathered back, as I sent my seeing spirit to peer through his steely eyes. Yet little did I think to be so nearly one with him as I have become, sitting high in the blue spaces, able to look afar with vision and more distantly with the inner sight.

In the years since I laid claim to this steep bit of the world, none has come this way to interrupt my thoughts or to disturb my dreaming. Looking into the why of being, up into the heavens, down into the deeps of earth, I have bound my still-rebellious flesh upon the wheel of discipline, and its iron has become a part of me. But I grew cold—cold and unfeeling, I fear, so that I often wondered if I still held the capacity to see through the eyes of another of humankind.

The winter just past was bitter, with snow piled to great depths and piercing winds fit to shatter the stones at the mouth of my cavern home. For those long months I was thrust within myself in earnest, wearing thin the speculations and philosophies which had seemed so strong and true in the freedom of summer. Memories arose unbidden to taint the clean heights with their polluted breath, and I again trod the paths of pain and anger which had led me to this refuge.

So, when the spring again crept to the high places, I was in no mood of spirit to welcome any who intruded upon my solitude. I walked the stony crags with old wrath still cankering my heart, and only slowly could the flower-scented breezes wash it clear.

There came a morning, clean as the first spring-dawn of the world, when I awoke to unease. I rose before the sun, pausing only to make a cup of broth to stay my hunger. Then I went onto the southern face of my pinnacle, picking my way carelessly among the stones, scanning always the southern lands which stretched in rolling billows beyond the view of eyes. Something was taking place, there at the edge of my perception, that I could feel as a fire along my nerves, as a tension in my bones. Wrath and death again walked near me—aye, and avarice and cruelty spurred them on, as always. I felt the bitter tang of despair and the sharp edge of doomed pride upon the wind, and I sat, waiting, among the rocks for the call that would send me forth.

Nothing was to be seen upon the pasturelands, nor could I hear those strange voices which wailed, at times, about the mountain's foot. All was stillness and peace and the calling of nesting birds amid the tender scents of young leaves and opening blossoms. Yet I was all unease, now standing to peer afar, now sitting to soak in the sun. Something there was within those peaceful lands which spoke to the old and warlike spirit that I had long ago quelled. So I waited through the forenoon, staying my hunger with provender from my pouch, never leaving my post.

Well into the afternoon, there came a change in the atmosphere. A tension crept up from the lowlands, and I seemed to hear, upon the edge of perception, the voices crying sadly in the pasturelands. Then, with a shattering suddenness, there came a summons, strong as the lightning-bolt upon the mountain, imperative, demanding, but without words, without pictures formed in the mind, simply a wild "I need!" sent screaming into the emptiness of the countryside.

I stood and hurried to gather from my cavern a pack with dried meat and fruits, together with the simple medicines which I compounded from stuffs at hand. Then I whistled, waiting with curiosity to learn if my lordly Wandir would gallop up from the meadows to answer that long-unheard summons. Long it was, and I began to descend the mountain, though knowing that any aid I might bring afoot might come too late to the caller in the grasslands. But Wandir met me upon the path and bowed his head to my hand. No saddle nor bridle did he ever bear, for we were friends and equals. I mounted him and turned his head in the direction of the call.

The lands rolled away beneath his steady hoofbeats, and before the sun touched the rim of the world I knew that we were near the spot I sought. By the wailing voices I knew it, and by the growing strength of the silent cry that drew me. Then I was surrounded by soft cries, moving through the air without the aid of any bodies which could be seen. No terror did they hold, but seemed welcoming, urging me on. I followed them, wondering that

Wandir did not fall into that shivering, snorting fear which such beasts are wont to show when spirits are about.

He moved steadily onward, seeming to follow the cries without my guidance. Just as the sun sank to rest, he stopped beside a stunted pine which stood alone in the broad expanses of pastureland. I dismounted, feeling truly the force of that will which had summoned me, and parted the low-swept branches to peer beneath.

Upon the needle-cushioned earth beneath the tree, I could see a human form, wrapped in a full robe. No answer did it make to my words, and I bent over closely to examine if this person be living or dead. Then I saw the bundle wrapped closely in its arms, and I knew the source of the call which had brought me from the mountain. It was not this woman who lay so deeply asleep, but the newly born child which she held who had summoned me.

No cry did he make, no sound, but eyes so darkly blue that they gave notice of their eventual blackness studied me intently, in a manner which I felt must be foreign, indeed, to the ways of those newborn. Under that strangely knowing gaze, I carefully woke the mother, who roused and sat in one motion, drawing from her robe a knife which she held as does one who knows its use.

"Nay, Lady," I said quietly. "I am no enemy, but only one brought forth from the mountains by the will of yonder child. Look upon me, robed in brown and unarmed save with thought, and you will know that I come upon no murderous mission."

Then she looked me full in the face, and the force contained behind those dark eyes brought me fully to awareness of the strangeness of her situation. How came one like this, obviously gently reared and tutored to the arts of survival, upon the wild lands, alone, with so young a child?

"Truly, you are none of those who follow us," she said at last, and her voice was ragged with anger, I thought, as much as with pain and grief. "I am Shanah of the house of Raithe—if such a family still endures." Then she told me what that day had brought to her and to hers, and I knew again the old fury growing within me, though I had thought it long ago ground into patience and acceptance.

"There will be those who ride after us," she warned me, when she finished her tale. "The horses of Raithe are of value to those who would war upon their neighbors and prey upon their own kind. We long ago scattered them where none else may find them, and they will be hot with anger and frustration. My folk have perished or fled by now, but the enemy knows that I escaped, and that I am —hindered—in my flight. So they will come. But Those Who Wait will harass them and frighten their horses and guide them astray, if it may be done. There may be time for you to save yourself."

"Some dealing have I had with such people, long before now," I replied. "I do not dread them. But you have the child to tend, and I may tend both until your strength returns. My Wandir is strong, and a double burden will not slow him overmuch. Let us move from this spot into the mountains, where I have a refuge which may baffle better trackers than any townsmen may become."

"My thanks to you," she said briefly. "There is no need to burden your mount, for I came upon my own, leading that of my husband. A few moments will bring them to us." And she whistled shrilly, twice.

I felt their hoofbeats in the earth beneath me before I heard them, and soon two horses such as I had never seen sped into my view. They were dark—dark as silvery smoke, with flowing gray manes and tails. They were saddled with soft leather and their bridles bore no bits, and their eyes told me that never had they been misused by any of humankind.

Straight to the tree they came and halted, nickering softly. Then Shanah spoke to them, and they quieted, standing firmly as I helped her to mount and settled the child in his carry-bag before her. Then I bestrode the mare, Plana, and whistled to Wandir, who must return the way he had come, and even more speedily. The grasslands seemed to melt before the hooves of those glorious steeds, and to roll away behind as we fled across the ways toward the sanctuary of the mountain.

Now the light was well-nigh lost from the sky, and there was no starlight, for ranks of cloud had come up from the western reaches and covered all the arc of heaven. We fled through blackness toward blackness, without any hope of seeing. Yet voices called ever before us, and our mounts followed them with perfect faith, and their hooves hammered a rhythm steadily from the unseen earth beneath.

Much did I wonder at the strangeness of the things which I had found at the source of my calling, but I could not ask my companion, for there was no hearing above the flowing of the wind past the ears. Often I strained to peer through the darkness to see how she fared, for she had seemed very weak when I helped her to mount her steed. Truly, I might as usefully have strained to see into a deep cavern without a torch; but the steady drum of the hooves had never faltered, as I felt sure they would have, had she fallen from her saddle.

Flying through those empty spaces, there was no reckoning of time, and long it seemed before the pace slackened and the horses eased into a brisk walk. Then I felt the nearness of the mountain before my face, and I smelled the cleanliness of the pine forest upon its heights. I whistled to Wandir, and soon he nuzzled at my leg, that I might know him near. Gentling Plana to a halt, I heard Gollas also come to rest, and I said, "We near my haven, and I must find torchwood and seek for the path. Wandir knows the ways well, and I shall let him lead us."

Shanah's voice was grown faint and thin, but she answered, "Seek you in my pack, behind you. There will be a lightglass there."

So I rummaged in the pack until I felt the slim shape that was the lightglass, and I set it upon my knee and spun the little wheel. Great cheer it gave my heart to see the shower of sparks give way to a blue flame which soon settled steadily into a yellow glow. Holding it high, I dismounted and climbed wearily onto Wandir's back, and we moved along the hem of the forest that cloaked the heights, seeking for the path which was so well hidden that few could find it by day, and only those familiar with the place could ever have located it in darkness.

At length, the twisted trunk of a lightning-smitten oak caught the light, and I led the horses toward it in triumph, for it marked the beginning of the path. Letting the others pass me, I dismounted again and went back along our track, erasing as best I could the mark of their passage, until I reached the grass we had just left. Then I backed away still brushing with the blanket I held, in order to remove my own prints.

Through a tangle which bore no evidence of being a path's beginning, we moved cautiously, the horses stepping high and delicately disengaging their hooves before taking the next step. Little trace was there that any had come this way, so far as I could tell by the feeble light of the glass. Then we moved beneath a hanging tapestry of vine, which swung down behind us, hiding our way from view of any who might come there by day.

Seldom had I ridden Wandir to the height, knowing that the steep way was difficult when he was over-balanced by a rider, and I did not now. But Shanah must ride, so I sent Wandir ahead up the path, and I strode behind, leading Gollas and hearing Plana following faithfully. Much was I concerned, as I saw her in the flicker from the lightglass, at the state of my charge, for she was paler than death, and will alone held her upon her mount. She had bound the bag which held the child tightly to the saddle, that she might better fend away the branches which brushed above the trail; that wonderful being swung in silence near my shoulder, his dark eyes catching the light, now and again, with never a sound of complaint.

No touch did I feel upon my spirit. He had called when there was need, and when there was none, he did not. Strange, strange. Totally unlike any infant ever known to me, he was red and wrinkled as any newly born babe, but

hunger and discomfort brought from him no cry. He
moved, as did his mother, to the working of will, not to
the naggings of flesh and emotion.

So we ascended, winding upward and upward along
the pathway. As we climbed, the voices which had led us
fell away behind, and there seemed in their cries a note of
farewell. Then there was only silence, and I turned my
eyes toward Shanah. She looked down from the place
where her grief and her exhaustion had taken her and
said, "They go southward again. Any who seek to follow
my track will find themselves . . . accompanied. The
horses of Raithe have no fear of them, nor does your
steed, who must pasture upon the flatlands that are their
home. But outland beasts fear them, as do their masters.
Aye, they go . . ." And her gaze turned back within herself, and she spoke no more.

Now we crossed a wide bed of scree, spread by an ancient landslip, and the horses snorted and set their hooves
with care, as the loose stuff slithered away underfoot and
went rattling down from the height. It was little easier to
tread the way in my skin shoes, but we all kept our foot-
ing, and with the passage of this last obstacle we found
ourselves drawing near to my cavern. With a word to
Shanah, I brought the horses to a halt and went within to
make light, which was speedily done with aid from the
flame in the lightglass.

Swiftly, I drew together a pile of skins and mosses from
my store and made a couch close beside the fire-stone,
where I kindled flame also. Then I led my strange guest
into my home and helped her to settle in comfort upon
the rude bed, with the child in the crook of her arm. She

drew him close and suckled him, as I went about freeing the beasts of their trappings and leading them to a nearby dell where grass grew thick and tender.

Upon my return, I found both soundly asleep, and I moved quietly as I mixed meat and dried fruits in my kettle and set it upon the hearth to simmer at the edge of the bed of coals. Then I lay down at ease upon my own couch and took rest, drifting into sleep in the warmth, with the scent of the stew in my nostrils comforting my spirit.

Sleep lasted only until the time before sunrise when the world listens. Then I woke, feeling within myself a stirring, as though a feather were being drawn across those senses which are attuned to the movements of others of my race. I rose to an elbow, ranging outward with those inner knowings. Out upon the long ways which we had crossed so swiftly, there moved men, seeking. That was to be expected, and my spirit confirmed it.

As I rose to replenish the fire, I saw that the eyes of my guests were open, those of the babe fixed upon me with speculation as interested as his mother's.

"They move in the grasslands," said Shanah, and there was no questioning in her voice. "The child also knows. I am no great seeker in spirit, but he has all the abilities of our family, for his father is also Raithe, and the talent has been doubled in him. To him I am attuned, and what he knows I catch as a shadow or an echo. We have brought the hunters near to your door. Think you that they may trace our way?"

"They are far, as yet," I answered. "And if they were at the mountain's foot, I think they would not know that any pathway exists, nor would they dream that you who were one now are three. Great rolls of highland begin at this ridge, and none could know by looking at them which would make safe refuge or even possible climbing. No, we are well enough, now. Let us bridle no uncaught horses."

She laughed and began again to suckle the child, and I set my pot to boil and moved about, tidying the bits of belongings which I had tossed about the cave. The loneliness of the past winter was now broken, and I could not sorrow at it. Old impulses began to awaken in my heart, and I could feel my blood move from its sluggish ways, my breathing came deep and strong, as if I were facing battle and possible death. Once again I, Lengalyon, was a living man, concerned with his kind, and the knowledge sang like wine along my veins.

Only for so long may one gnaw upon the bones of old wrongs and drink the cup of past bitterness. There comes a point past which the spirit starves if it finds no newer sustenance. Now there was strong meat set before me, and I was glad.

Strong tea of pine tips I now brewed, and Shanah and I fell to upon the stew I had set to simmer upon our arrival. I had rolled away the stone at the cavern mouth, and the sweet air of the spring rolled in, bearing with it the cleanliness of the fir-scented air and the breath of young leaves and new blossoms. With such sauce, our fare seemed rich indeed, and we ate slowly and with contentment, smiling at one another now and again. The child slept quietly beside us, and there seemed no terror in all the world.

But soon enough the meal ended, and my guest insisted upon clearing away the remains and making all neat again. Truly she was a strong woman, though I could see that she was still sore and exhausted from the many ordeals of the day just past. As she moved about, she seemed to gain strength and suppleness, and the color began to come again to her tawny skin.

After a bit, I rose and went to look over the lowlands, knowing that she needed time alone to tend herself. She smiled when I bade her good-bye, and I saw a flash of the lovely creature she was. I hoped in my soul that her Raf had contrived to live, that he might bring that light often to her eyes. His son, also, would have need of a father, and I felt a little envy of a man so fortunate as to have wedded such a wife and sired such a child.

The shadow of old grief brushed me as I stole through the forest toward my southern observation post. My lost ones seemed near at hand, almost tangible, and I was comforted by the notion, though it had never been so before. My son—would no longer be a babe, but a man grown. My La-ni would be gray, even as I, but always beautiful. Perhaps in some remote bourne of the gods they sought to relieve my sorrow, yet in my self-wrapped bitterness I could not feel or know their concern. Now my armor of self was undone, and the healthful winds of spring and change were winnowing out my fusty spirit, that I might again be a whole man. I drew myself straight and stepped among the stones as surely as a goat or a hart.

But when I came to the beginning of the bare slopes to southward, I lay upon my face and wriggled forward, keeping ever behind rock and scrub. Well was it that I did, for when I at last ventured to peer out into tho grasslands, there were dust-streaks upon the horizon, and

I knew that men scoured the countryside, seeking Shanah. From the aimlessness of the signs, it was apparent that they followed no trail, but quartered the lowlands, searching for traces.

I smiled deep in my beard, for I knew that none might pick our trail from the maze of tracks left there by the flocks of wild goats and cattle that browsed even to the lower parts of the mountain. Not by riding their mounts lame might they come upon the lair of so old and experienced a fox as I. Those were no mountainbred hounds yonder, but men with wits blunted by lives spent elbow-to-elbow with their fellows. Such are those who play the pawn to such as the man who now sits upon the high place at Lirith.

I felt, though I did not hear, the approach of my guests and turned to see how Shanah came into the exposed places. But I should have known that she would come as a shadow slipping down the slope, with the child in his bag at her shoulder. She said nothing as she settled behind a neighboring stone, but her eyes were bright and fierce, and I could feel the intense interest that was the infant breaking about my mind as a wave.

Perhaps I should now examine in my heart the truth of that which was Shanah's son. Knowledge he had not—how could he, at less than a day of age? Yet he had . . . intuition? Not quite. Consciousness of impending danger to himself. Yes, and interest which cut like a knife through space and spirit, seeking. He saw and knew, somewhat, through his mother's eyes and mind, and thus had advanced far beyond any babe I had ever heard of. But he ranged afar, unerringly, in the direction from which his own peril came, and this spoke of a spirit which likely was unequalled among our kind in all its days.

Silent, we lay in the good sunlight, watching the plains below. The specks which were men on horseback began to separate themselves from the dust-trails, and we could see how they cast back and forth across the land, a long line of men spread widely. I opened my spirit and sent it outward, feeling with gladness that my companions had no panic in them. Fear there was, and pain, and courage fit to melt good steel, and they sent my seeking sense upon its way in good cheer.

But it was otherwise when I reached the ranks of men. Anger boiled there, and quaking terror fit to send them mad. Then I looked through the eyes and listened through the ears of one, and I understood. Those Who Wait cried about them, wailing the air thick, sending the horses half-wild. I remembered Shanah's tale, and I was well pleased with the work of her longfathers.

Narrative of Ruthella ni Raithe do Naill

Not the strongest, nor the bravest, nor the best of my folk
am I. None ever called me so, nor did I claim to be. But I
have found myself to be tough and tenacious of life beyond my expectations or wishes. Who would dream that
my quiet life of house-tending and wifehood might create
within me a warrior, huntsman, a survivor in the wild?

Fear walked with me into morning, upon the last day
spent within the walls of Fallowden. I gazed upon my
Millis, knowing it to be the last time that I would see his
proud head flaming high in the old rooms. When I held
him at the doorway, he looked into my eyes and said,
"Whatever come, Ownling, we have known joy together.
Living or dying let us never forget it, but hold it before
us as a candle to light the way into whatever unknown
lies before us."

Then I looked up at him and said, "Know, my love, that
I may hold your child. Not certainly, but mayhap. If it
should be that I live and you perish, that one shall know
pride in his father." My reward was the flare of happiness
that kindled within him as the spark in a lightglass. He
went out into the orchard to join our kin and his back
was straight and his step was light as though he walked to
tend the fruit trees. I watched until the last ruddy flash of

light glanced from his hair as he sank into concealment.
Then I slammed the great doors and ran the bars through
the grooves.

We waited through the long morning. Our brothers
came from the far ways where they had chivied the
enemy upon the road, and they kissed us and saluted the
Raithe and Shanah, then were away to the wall, where
they sank, invisible, behind the shrubbery. I again barred
the doors upon the brightness of the spring day, and listened against the panels for the clamor which spoke of
the enemy's approach.

When that first rush brought the shouting and the ring
of metal weapons before our door, I drew my sword and
stood before the doorway, ready. But they brought a ram
against the panels, and my grandsir ordered me back. I
found myself reluctant, though my knees shook and my
teeth rattled against one another, seek as I might to hold
them tight-clenched.

But when the door gave, and I saw the armored form of
an outlander darken the gap, I felt an awful rage that
such as he should set his heel upon our land. My sword
met him as he sought to enter the hall and slipped
sweetly between his ribs. Then I fought with such fury
that I cannot remember how many I slew and I never
felt the wounds that were given me. Often one whom I
was measured against fell at my feet, skewered with a
black-feathered arrow, and I knew that Shanah still held
her post at the stairhead. The Raithe was grunting as he
heaved his mace, and its shattering crunch came regularly
as a pendulum. Talitha I found beside me, and well she
acquitted herself; for her lances bristled in more than one

of those upon whom we trod in the press of the battle, and her sword was busy.

I saw Talitha slain, and I turned to my grandsir, standing beside him to guard his back. There was a lull about us as new warriors forced through the entryway and rushed the stair, but I believe that Shanah had fled. And then they turned again to us two. Desperately I parried as swords swung at me. I felt a blow upon my side as my foot turned beneath me. Then there was only darkness.

I woke to silence. Death would be silent, I thought, but I listened, listened, and then I heard the twitter of the graybird in the lilac before our riven door. Then feeling began to return, and I wondered at the terrible weight that lay over me. At last I dared to open my eyes, and I found myself lying twisted against the wall. The Raithe lay upon me, his great form blocking out all view of the hall, save for a narrow space next the floor. Through that gap I could see his hand still grasping the mace.

There was a sharp pain beneath my left arm, and many stabs of anguish from other spots. But my great need was to be free of my grandsir's weight, that I might straighten my cricked bones and find what I might do to aid myself. Squirming, I set my back against the wall and drew up my knees, then pushed against his tremendous shoulders with my feet. With a sighing sound, he began to move. He toppled over onto his face, and I could see his white hair streaked with blood where some fell blow had split his helm.

I sat against the wall, gasping, looking upon what had been my home. Blood dried upon the flagstone floor, though the enemy had taken his dead with him when he withdrew. Talitha lay upon her back across the stairway, and her throat had been cut, though I knew that she had died from a sword-thrust through the body. Then I saw how the gods had shielded me with the body of the Raithe, hiding me from those who might have served me so, had they been able to see me.

Rising with many a halt and groan, I struggled to the kitchen and cleansed my wounds with water, binding them with bandages that we had made together in the winter against this very need. Tears came, though not many, as I made myself as fit as possible.

Then I made my painful way up the stair, to see if my sister lay above. But of her there was no sign, and the panel had been drawn inside the bolthole, so I knew that she had fled safely. I laid my head against the panel and willed that the gods might aid and shelter her, for well I knew that her time was very near. I did not try to go the way she had gone. Likely it was that our invaders now were scouring the grasslands to the north, suspecting that our horses might be concealed there. I must make my way a different one and leave no trace nor trail to guide any after me.

There was no time to care for the bodies of my dear ones, but I straightened their limbs and covered their faces with linen. Then I went out into the orchard, making certain that no watcher had been left to observe the house before I slipped into the hedges that led me round-about to my goal.

Between the flowering trees a grave had been dug, large enough for many men, and I knew that it held the bodies of our slain enemies. But our own dead—their bod-

ies had been hung from an old apple tree. And there was
my Millis, with the sun glinting still on his red hair. Eris
and Irian bore him company. But of Raf and Perrin there
was no sign, and I held hope in my heart that they had
escaped.

Now I was cold, and no sorrow came near me—only an
icy anger that wrapped me round and held all hurt away.
With my belt knife, I cut down our three dear ones and
laid them side by side in the grasses, looking at the sky
amid a tender rain of pink and white petals. Let any who
might come read the message. One—at least—of the
Raithes of Fallowden yet lived. Well might the knowledge serve them, for I intended to leave no more foot-
print in my path than a spirit or one of Those Who Wait.
And I stood beside the body of my husband and I cursed
Him Who Sits at Lirith with all the cold fire which the
gods had lent to me.

My carefully prepared bags of supplies still waited in
their places. Though I had no mount, I shouldered two of
them and set out across the grasslands to the eastward,
keeping to patches of short grass and using such stunted
trees and bushes as there were for cover, though there
was little need. The sun was now set and twilight made it
hard to see anything at a distance. Yet I was not prepared
to stop until Fallowden sank into the edge of the sky, so I
forced my stiffening muscles forward, holding to the pain
of my wounds as a goad to spur me onward.

When it grew too dark to walk with safety, I halted and
sank into a little grassy runnel that crossed my path. It
was now dry, for only the winter's snows used it for
runoff, and it dipped deeply enough for me to feel that I

might safely make a small fire, for I knew that I must not chill deeply, or I might never rise again. A clump of twisted pine scrub provided fuel, sorry enough, but sufficient when kindled with twists of the past winter's grasses, together with dried cones. The little flame, banked round with stones, made a pocket of warmth and light beneath the terrible emptiness that was this night's sky, and I huddled in the blankets from the packs, nibbling upon the tasteless food, sipping from the water bottle, thawing that frozen interior again into a semblance of myself.

As Ruthella ni Raithe I was born. As Ruthella ni Raithe do Naill I lived my happy years at Fallowden. And as Ruthella—at least—I must finish out my life and make a way for my child, if one there was to be. That being of ice that I had become for a time was a thing of fear to me. Better to be wracked with the bitter grief of loss, winnowed by the winds of passions, than to live in that frozen state. So I sat before the little fire beneath the cold sky and told myself that Millis was dead. My folk were dead or scattered beyond my reach. My home was foreclosed to me for a space, perhaps forever. None could I call upon, to none could I look for aid.

Desolation seized me. For a time I sat in emptiness, feeling the world about me as a void and this small spot as the only bit of unshaken earth in all space. But tears did not come. Millis did not remain in that cold clay in the orchard. He was, but elsewhere. Perhaps he now wandered with Those Who Wait, or he might be with the gods in their strange places. But always he would be with me. And therein lay my strength. Let me live or die; yet I

would be with my own in spirit, and his steadfastness
would bear me wherever I must go.

Warmed and comforted, I fell asleep, and the night
brought no ill dream, no dark terror to my heart. I was
wrapped in pride and honor, and I felt the nearness of my
folk as I drifted into the darkness.

I wakened abruptly to early day and the thudding vibration of hooves, inaudible as yet, but borne through the
earth to my ear as I lay upon the ground. I rose swiftly
and covered over the dead ashes of my fire. Then I sank
into the runnel and peered cautiously over the edge,
screened by the scanty grasses and bushes.

No galloping figure was yet within seeing, but the hoofbeats grew in volume until they were sound as well as
feeling inside the bones. Then I saw, back to the westward, a handful of horsemen come fleeing out of the
northeastern horizon, clinging desperately to steeds gone
wild and uncontrollable. I cocked my head and listened.
Then I smiled, though my face came near to splitting
with the effort. The familiar voices came down the spring
breeze, wailing fit to madden better beasts than those
upon the plain. Those Who Wait had turned a party
which, in searching for our Fallowden horses, had come
too near to the true direction. No Raithe ever born, whatever his present condition, would let our hooved kindred
be led beneath the yoke of such masters.

No mere dream had led me into sleep yesternight. My
folk had been near, even as I had felt, and they were even
now about their fated task of caring for their own.
Mayhap even Millis himself moved yonder with our people, still carrying on the battle which his flesh had been

forced to abandon. I thought of his laughing face beneath the flaming crest of hair, and tears of grief and of joy and of weakness rose in my eyes. But I blinked them back sternly and went about gathering my blankets neatly into the packs, that I might move quickly into the eastern valleys.

The sun was little above the horizon as I began to move again across the grasslands. The long slant of its beams ran across the land, making tall shadows for weed and stone and stunted tree alike. My own elongated shade stepped along behind me, and I wished with all my spirit that I were as great and fearless as that tall shape. If only Shanah strode beside me, secure in her fearless confidence. For her the sky would be peopled with no faces of those she had slain. Often I have envied my young sister for her straightforward and untroubled heart. If she had been forced to kill, it was by no choice of hers, and no dead eyes would ever regard her reproachfully from shadow and sky. What she did, she did, and never did she look back.

But for me there was no such ease of heart. Faces that I had not consciously seen as I stabbed and slashed now peered at me from stone and shrub, and I felt again the deadly whip of the sword in my hand and the strange feel of a blade slipping into flesh. All our early training had set our bodies at ease in such work, but for the spirit there could be no prior hardening. I wept, as I struggled across the plain, for those whom I had slain more than for those of mine who lay dead.

But the day wore to noon, and tears had an end. The night had stiffened my wounds, making travel harder than before. Only will and unceasing effort kept my feet moving upon the way. After a time, I moved through a fog of pain and weariness that wrapped me in a cocoon, and I seemed to drift forward like a mist toward the ridged hills which were now visible above the horizon.

Not in one day, nor in two, did I reach those comforting slopes, but a day came when I found myself among the pine thickets that rose about their lower parts. Then I woke from the dazed state which had enclosed me, and I knew that I was near to my goal. New vigor entered my limbs, and I pushed forward, circling about the giant knees of tree-grown eminences keeping always my face to the east.

When the first of our Fallowden horses came within my sight, I felt tears come into my eyes. I raised my voice in the Raithe call; the distant smoky shape flung up its head and flowed into motion. As he neared, I saw that it was Perrin's stallion Fallon, and he loped easily to my side and bent his great head to gaze at me with wonder and recognition. I touched his mane and clung, burying my face in the familiar scent and texture of his coat.

He stood patiently, and I grew calmer and spoke to him, fondling him. He nickered softly with pleasure and made no objection as I laid the packs, now tied together, across his back and crawled painfully after them, setting my left toe behind his knee to aid my climb. By the pressure of my knees, I turned him toward the east, and then I gave him his head. His misty mane brushed my face as he swung along, and soon I could see other horses grazing about the small green valley that unfolded before us.

They raised their heads and whinnied, and I called to them all in the horse-talk of Raithe.

In a moment, we were surrounded by that loving throng. They walked sedately about us, and we moved together down into the valley, across its grassy expanse, and up into the pinewood that lapped the farther side. Well had Raf and Shanah chosen this refuge. Many new colts squealed and raced about upon their knobby-kneed and spindly legs. The mares were sleek and contented, and the geldings and the yearlings romped together in the distance, nipping at one another and kicking up their heels with well-being.

When Fallon reached the wood, he stopped and looked over his shoulder at me, telling me plainly as any word could do that this was the place where I should get down. And truly it was a sheltered spot, tucked against a rocky bluff and ringed about with tall pines, whose branches swept low, almost to touch the earth. I slid stiffly to earth, clinging to the stallion's mane until I felt able to stand.

The packs slipped down easily enough, and I dragged them over the smooth mat of needles and placed them in a cranny against the face of the bluff. There was a flat stone lying like a hearth, and upon it I kindled a fire. I found the light cookpot which I had placed in the pack and poured into it water from my bottle, knowing that I could follow the horses to their spring later.

While dried meat simmered beside the blaze, I rested, not sleeping, but totally relaxed, feeling myself again with friends and family. And truly, the hooved ones came, singly and in groups, to poke their soft noses into my hand and to nuzzle at my ear or my hair, as if they rejoiced again to have their own with them. So near have we always been, horse with Raithe and Raithe with horse, that no mere passage of time, unless it be for generations, could dull the love which we feel.

So I went to earth among the horses of Fallowden, biding in the hills and using the fruits of the soil and the small beasts of the forest for my food. A brush hut I built against the cliff to which Fallon had brought me, and there I lived, but not in loneliness. What time I did not spend in adding to my store of food, I used for teaching the yearlings to bear a rider, to come at call, to stand when bidden, all the arts which Raithes have schooled into their steeds for generations uncounted. The foals I gentled, making them my playfellows.

No, I was not lonely, and if my dreams were lit by a crest of flaming hair, it did not sadden me, for I felt always in a corner of my heart the assurance that my Millis was not completely lost to me, and that my folk were ever mindful of me, spirit calling to spirit across the rift of death.

Narrative of Him Who Sits at Lirith

The winds of destiny, though fickle and chancy, may be caught and tamed to the will of a man with strength and daring enough to attempt their harnessing. Such a one have I ever been, ready to reach out my hand for any opportunity. Those who call me cruel and conscienceless have never been moved by fate to the heights of power and dominion, as have I, and cannot know that they would not have done just as I, had they been placed so.

Strength of will and the ability to dominate those of influence and family aided me in creating a following in Lirith which I used cunningly to place men of mine in positions of importance in the government of the city. Thus, when the illness and death of the First Minister of our country created an interruption in the flow of power, I was able to step into that breach and, with the aid of those whom I had placed in high offices, take into my own hands the governance of all Kyrannon.

No bloody revolution did I foment, no destructive and rampageous war that would have flattened towns and cities and destroyed the wealth of the nation. No, I quietly and humanely severed a few unusually stubborn heads from their owners' bodies, and thereafter I dwelt in peaceful control of all the land about. None dared to raise his voice against me, and all quaked at my frown and basked in the warmth of my favor. For long I was content.

Then there came to my ears talk of the land to the south and east of Kyrannon, a fair country of busy seaports and much wealth. Little interest had the rulers of Gryphos in their neighbors, being immersed in the business of trade with lands across the seas and the amassing of riches beyond belief. Yet inquiry determined that such store of wealth there was, and I thought long. Never had the nations of this continent warred, being divided by chains of mountains and great expanses of plains that made the carrying on of warfare an unprofitable process. But for such wealth as there was to be had for the taking, surely one might devise a way to seize it, thus making the folk of my own nation more secure and happy, with only small expenditure of lives and gold as the cost.

Privately I talked with many who traveled afar, and with those who had dwelt long in Lirith, as well, winnowing from their memories all that I could learn of the resources at my command. Much I learned and long I thought upon my gleanings, and I found, to my displeasure, that there were those within the boundaries of Kyrannon who possessed treasures and steeds valuable to their country, but who did not own the sway of any ruler at Lirith. True, they lived far from the city, across the grasslands to the north, the mountains to the west, and the country to the south near the border of Gryphos, but this did not excuse them from their duty of sending tribute to their rightful overlord.

Stiff-necked and wrongheaded folk they seemed, all of them, but those who most irritated my sense of fitness were those of the house of Raithe, in the northland. More than one ruler who had sat in my chair had reached out his hand to bring them to obedience, and their great horses to his service, and never had they submitted. Many had perished, indeed, battling those who had the right to govern them, and many more had disappeared for long spans of time; but ever had they crept back into their old place and ways when time had made it safe for them.

Even so, they might have been ignored and permitted to live, well away from any in whom they might foment rebellion, had they not refused to pay tribute to their ruler. Their horses, so I was told, were faster, stronger, more intelligent and enduring than any ever seen elsewhere. But so jealous were they of those beasts that they would only sell or barter them to one whom they examined closely as to his temper and moral ways. None would they let from their hands to any whom they suspected of cruelty. And none whatever would they send to their sovereign, who might choose to allot them to those who pleased him, without first questioning them as to their treatment of their animals. Yet I dealt fairly with them, to begin. I brought their agent before me and gave the opportunity for them to sell to me enough of their beasts to mount a troop of cavalry.

The man quailed before me, fawning and shivering, yet he could only say, "There is no possible way in which the Raithe could be persuaded to sell his horses for war, Lord. If it were to be done, I should take the road myself, this moment. Yet I know, from long dealing, that the old man who rests at Fallowden will not. What can I say to you?" And he fell to shaking and twisting his cap into a string of leather.

I took no vengeance upon him, for I pride myself upon my fairness of mind. But when I dismissed him, I knew that I would have horses from Fallowden, come what might. For I had not really foreseen that I might purchase those beasts, nor did I truly wish to. Such overly independent folk must be chastened, if a man is to sit securely in his place of power, and their stubbornness now could justly bring about their downfall.

So I summoned Tharan, the commander of cavalry, and told him my wish.

Much to my astonishment, he paled. Even his hands went waxen, and he looked at me with what seemed sheer terror in his eyes.

"Lord, I live to do your will," he said at last. "Yet hear me. I have lived upon the nearer edge of the grasslands, in my youth. Somewhat I know of the Raithes of Fallowden, and of Those Who Wait upon the lands about them. I will not say that this task is impossible, for that none can say until he tries. But I know that it is unlikely . . . most unlikely . . . that those who ride out to perform it will return unscathed, or at all."

"Are they so many and so fierce, these Raithes, that trained troops need fear them?" I asked sarcastically. "Surely, with your many tens of men, you may overcome them with little effort."

"Not many are they," he replied, "and some of them women, though not such women as we breed in the towns. Neither are they fierce by nature. Rather are they shy of outlanders and loving of their own. But they are trained from birth to fight for their family, their home, and their horses; and fight they do, by old report, until the last falls or is forced to flee. They are foemen worthy of the best. But not even this is the terror of Raithe. For thereabout, upon the lands where their horses graze, there are those who cry from invisible mouths, wail upon the winds, sending the heart into pounding fear, blinding the eyes with panic, maddening the horses that we must ride there. Once I rode among them, when I lost myself in a snowstorm, and never will I forget the near-madness which they brought to me."

He fell silent, and I could see in his eyes the remnant of old fear. Nonetheless, I handed him my warrant, sealed and stamped, and said, "Still, we must bring these folk to heel. Slay them if you must, or bring any who survive as captives to me. Gather together all their horses, that we may mount an army for war."

I could see him brighten, as I had thought he would. One trained for war is never content until he has exercised his craft, and he was no exception.

"Between us two alone," I continued, "I may speak of this, but let it not be rumored abroad; for war is a serious step, not to be undertaken until all is prepared and the minds of the people are readied for it."

Then I smiled at him, as if including him in the fellowship of those who are able to sway men, and he drew himself straight as a lance and said, "We shall accomplish your purpose, Lord. We ride immediately for Fallowden."

It is so easy to manipulate ordinary men. One wonders that more do not discover the way, and so make themselves kings and conquerors.

Narrative of Perrin dir Raithe

No man of words, I, nor have I ever easily laid tongue to seemly phrases. Yet now I must carry forward the tale of my folk, seeking to make clear those happenings which passed within my ken.

Upon the morning of battle, I, with my brothers and my sisters' men, sheltered within the wall of the orchard; and when the horses of the enemy halted without the gate we rained arrows upon them without mercy. Then many of the foemen fell wounded or slain, and we drew back into the garden to avoid their answering hail of lances.

With noise and outcry, they were upon us, and I saw Eris fall, pierced by a lance. Then I was forced back, through the garden and into the farther part of the orchard, beset by three swordsmen. One I slew with the shortsword in my left hand, and then I was put to it to hold the two remaining from draining my lifeblood away into the grass. Twice they slipped beneath my guard, driving deeply into my side and my hip; yet I was able to stand and to hold my sword, and I overcame them at last.

But when I turned to go again into the garden, I felt the light fade within my eyes, and I fell. Only strength had I to crawl away into the barberry bushes, drawing my feet up close, that they might not show to any who came seeking after me. Then there was only nothingness for a long, long time.

I opened my eyes to a night so dark that I thought it death indeed. No sound was there save the faint brush of the wind among the leaves, and no light shone from the house. Still, I struggled to rise and, finding that I could not, crawled to the door and into the hall of Fallowden. Then I found strength to stand and, mindless of danger, I lit the lightglass that stood within the niche of the entryway and stood looking about at the working of our enemies. My grandsir lay within the hall, his great bulk stretched at length, his mace within his hand, as though he still defended his own. Across the foot of the stair lay Talitha, and I felt tears rise in my eyes at the loss of them. Then I saw that their faces were covered with linen. So. One of my folk lived, I knew then, and I grinned at the thought.

In the kitchen I found the store of bandage and healing salves and saw that one had been there before me. Much time it took to clean away the crusted blood and remove my clothing, that I might tend my wounds. Washed and wrapped, I went up the stair, clinging to the railing and moaning with every step. No trace was there of Shanah, nor of Ruthella, and hope lit within me that even three of the family might be left to send vengeance down upon Him Who Sits at Lirith.

I found within my chamber fresh clothing and a pack of supplies for journeying. No sign was there that the enemy had yet pillaged, and I thought that they were so hot upon the trail of our horses that they had saved the smaller thievery for last. Thus I knew that I must go, and swiftly, before they returned to give the house their attention.

With the pack across my good shoulder, I walked out of the house of my people and went out upon the wildlands, turning to the west, where none of our folk had ever gone. If I must be sent out, well it would be to see new things and to meet mayhap, folk unlike those we had known. But the darkness was very thick, and no star pierced the clouds to light my path. When I had gone a fair distance from Fallowden, I found a patch of tall grass and burrowed into it to sleep out the time until sunrise.

I woke to hoof-thunder. Distant it was, yet carried to me through the earth, and I sat up in my grassplot to look about. First light was in the sky, and the sun would soon rise. I gazed far toward the east, and at length I saw specks grow upon the horizon that became men mounted upon beasts, as they drew nearer. Riding as madmen, they passed upon the farther side of Fallowden and were lost to sight. Then I set my chin in my hand and chuckled. No need had I to be near to know what it was that so frightened man and beast, out upon the grasslands. Those Who Wait were there, tending their own, as always they had and would. I had only to keep watch to avoid the path of such as those riders, for little pursuit would there be, I was willing to wager.

Stiff I was when I rose to go again westward, and each step was pain that tried the will. Even with fresh wrappings and new application of ointments, the wounds seemed near to festering. Yet I moved toward my goal, those distant mountains that none of mine had ever explored. Sometimes the sun swam strangely in the sky, and sometimes the earth rocked gently as they say the ocean may do. Once I found myself stretched upon the earth, without memory of how I came there.

Doubtful it is that I would ever have reached those westward marches, had not the gods, with their usual unexpected attentiveness, provided aid. When night fell, I also fell and slept where I lay in the grass. I woke to a familiar sound, and I rolled over to see if I had only dreamed that a horse was cropping the grass near to my head. Truly, there he stood, a gelding with the lather of running dried upon his coat, his face wearing that sorrowful expression of one used to servitude who is left suddenly masterless. He favored his left forefoot, and I thought it likely that he had stepped into a hole while flying from Those Who Wait on the day before. Most likely, that was also where he lost his master.

Quietly I sat, taking my time, and he did not shy away. Then I reached into my pack and drew out the salt bag. With a little salt in my hand, I began inching toward him, still sitting. He raised his head and looked at me, whiffling his nostrils and cocking his ears forward. When he reached his neck out toward my hand, I stopped as I was and let him come to me. And he did. He nuzzled his nose into my hand and licked away the salt, then bumped my shoulder, wanting more. Whatever his allegiance, the master had been a man who made a friend of his steed. And well did that serve me, for the beast was not afraid of mankind, and I was able to stand and take his bridle, easing the bit that he might eat more readily.

The saddle that he wore was a great chairlike thing, hung all about with weapons and supplies. I cut the girth and let it slip to the ground, and then I saw the long cut on his barrel. Some unlucky sword-stroke had missed its target, and he had suffered for it. With my salves, I tended the wound and stitched it closed with sewing gear from the pack. My blessing went out to Ruthella, wherever she might be, for her forethought and industry.

So I had found aid, and a friend to travel with. I could not ride him, for his hurts were too great, but my pack went across his back, well forward of the cut, and I walked beside, leaning my weight against him when the sky darkened, clinging to his mane when we moved forward. And we went with fair speed, for two lame things. Day became night and night day, without my caring or counting, and fever dimmed my thought, but the mountains grew taller. One day they were green and not blue, and I knew we drew near to them.

The horse found a creek that flowed from the heights, and we followed its narrow valley up and up. Past the trees we went, onto high and stony places. One day we looked down into a valley so green and tender and inviting that we stood gazing for a long time, unable to believe what we saw. We stopped that night in a pocket of rock surrounded by junipers. There had been a fire built there before. We used the stone for our own, and the fragrant juniper smoke stung our eyes. Food was a great need, but I found that I could neither cook nor eat the cold provender. Then I looked up at the horse and said, "My friend, you have brought me to a fair place, a place where we could have been safe and happy. Yet I have come as far as I may. Here I must stay to wait for death, but you must go on, down into that green valley, and grow fat and live long."

He hung his great head over me, as if he understood, and his eyes were sad. But I could only touch his nose once more and lay my head back against the rock.

Then I seemed to have strange dreams. One who seemed clothed in fur came and looked at me with unhuman eyes and spoke. Though he seemed to have language, I could not understand, for it sounded like whimpers and hisses and little hoots. I smiled, and he disappeared in grayness. Then another came and touched my hand. I opened my eyes, then opened them wider, for it seemed that my friend the horse had become a man, almost. Or a man had become a horse. Golden eyes he had, and a roached mane of hair down his neck, and pointed ears which he could twitch forward. Yet he spoke in the tongue of men, and he said, "I shall take you to the Wise One. Have no fear. We will lift you, and you will feel pain, but we will bear you to one who heals."

I nodded, and they lifted me. There was only pain, greater or lesser, for long after that.

I lay for many days in a hazed restfulness, warm and comforted and fed, but for a time I did not know who cared for me, or why. There came a day when my unfocused eyes again reached clarity, and I looked upon a room where wood met wood at corner and ceiling and floor, all aglow with firelight that touched its mellow surfaces. No stone was there, except for the hearth, and the floor was matted with bright rugs, the small windows hung with bright draperies of a nubby weave.

Used to the forest and the plain and the comfortable
austerity of Fallowden, I found this little room pleasant to
a new sense, which I had not been conscious of possess-
ing.

I had observed and absorbed all my surroundings
within sight when there came a step without the door.
Eager to see who would enter, I tried to rise upon my
elbow, but found that I could not. Still, I turned my head
so that I could see the doorway. There stepped into my
vision a lady in gray, small and slender but with the qual-
ity of strength surrounding her as it surrounds a fine
blade of steel. She was not very young, though her face
was unlined and her movements easy and supple as a
child's. But from her eyes there looked long-seasoned
wisdom and much kindness and sternness that could, I
surmised, become frightening.

She smiled. "I find you waking to reason, friend Perrin," she said.

I gaped in wonder. "How, then, know you my name,
Lady?" I stammered.

"Long have we held you in our care, my son. You have
spoken in delirium. Also, we know from mind to mind,
having that power, my daughter and I. We have seen the
ruin of your house, the murder of your folk, your flight—
all as it returned to your fevered spirit as your wounds
cleansed themselves of their poison."

"But how came I to you?" I asked. "I thought I
dreamed . . ."

"The People of the Heights saw you come to rest, and
they oversaw you. From late experience, they have reason
to distrust strangers, but they felt the bond between you

and the beast which came with you. Much they know of
what takes place in the hearts of beings which bear the
burden of reason, and they knew they need not fear you.
So they called to the Wildings, who came from their
forested places to bear you to me, whom they know to be
the only healer in their small world."

"The Wildings . . . like a horse, but more like a man?" I
asked.

"Aye. Their longfathers most like bore four hooves in
the beginning, before the tides of change diverted them
from their old paths. They are gentle folk, straying seldom
from their glades and thickets."

There came another tapping of steps in the passage,
and she turned. "Now you must meet my daughter, who
is called Cara. Like her father she is to look upon, but her
heart resembles mine."

A very young woman now entered the chamber, and
she was tall and fair and her eyes were gray. She carried a
basin, very carefully so as not to spill the contents, and
she came to the side of the bed and set it upon the little
table there, before she turned her eyes to me.

"Good day to you, Perrin dir Raithe," she said, and
there was laughter behind her solemn greeting. "So we
find you recovered in your wits today? You have been so
wandering, if you would believe, that you have always
addressed me as Your Graciousness as though I were of
the high blood, and my mother as Sir. It is well to set you
aright." Then she laughed indeed as the blood rushed to
my face.

But I saw that she was making merry, and I laughed
with her as she took my hands in hers and washed them

in the steaming basin and wiped them dry upon a towel. Then her mother brought forward a smaller bowl whose rich fragrance set my nostrils dancing. This I was able to empty, to their evident satisfaction, and with smiles they left me to rest.

I did not sleep, but lay in comfort, thinking of the strange fortune which had brought me from horror unspeakable into a place of lovely magics. Then I thought of the horse, and I knew that I must find news of that faithful beast. Looking about, I saw upon the table a small handbell, which I took up and tinkled. In a moment the steps came again, and Cara entered.

"You have need?" she asked.

"The horse . . . did he follow us? I would know how he fares," I answered.

"Well," she said. "Look from the window." And she pulled aside the drapery that I might see from the window.

In the bit of smooth grass visible over against the encircling forest of strange silver-gray-foliaged trees stood my friend. Cara whistled between her teeth, and he raised his head and trotted over to the casement, peering inside. With joy I spoke to him, and he whiffled softly in reply.

I let my head fall back to the pillow, feeling white exhaustion wash over me. Then Cara closed the curtain and moved beside me, lifting me to drink some tart and warming brew that sent me into sleep.

Narrative of Cara

Strange times have come upon this valley where moon-trees grow. For year upon year we walked, my mother and I, uncompanioned in the forest and on the height, speaking only one with the other, or with the Wildings and the People of the Heights. But none of humankind set his foot here, save only we two. As if some magic had been set about in a great bubble, no outsider ever came, no rumble of the trials of the folk overmountain ever penetrated so far as to catch our ears or to set our seeing senses questing.

Then, as if some warlock spoke a word, the bubble misted away, and the world came into this place where we have lived so long untroubled. First there came Heraad, who killed for joy and sport. Upon him Tisha and I exerted our wills, and him we sent forth to trouble us no more, leaving us very thoughtful. For in the working of this force between us we found a power so potent as to be frightening, even to us who are versed in the uses of the spirit.

In the year after his departure, we exercised, together and apart, that talent of the mind which so few of our kind seem to possess. We learned to move stones and timbers through the air, though the labor was no less than that in our old way of hauling them by hand or upon our cart. We each, secretly to begin, learned to cast darts and arrows with terrible force for great distances, holding in the eye of the heart a target. And we found that we could pierce that unseen target with a bolt far from eyeshot. Then we boasted of our feats and found that both had feared the same. The world, having learned the way to our door, might not be content to let that path remain unused.

So we feared another intruder, and we armed ourselves with weapons which might not be wrested from our hands. Thus, when a Wilding came in haste through the forest to our door, we felt within his mind the shape of an outlander, and we were troubled. None must be judged before he is seen, however, and we consented to have the man brought to us; for the Wilding said that he was sorely wounded and ill, as though he had been long unfed and his wounds untended.

And he was ill—terribly so—for many days. But in his sickness he spoke, and we listened, and we felt within his heart for the truth of his being. We found him strong and honest and unafraid, though he had walked through tragedy with his folk. Even when his mind wandered amid bloodshed and death, he spoke no untoward word, though we were able to follow the course of his battle step by step as he fought it once again. Stern and clean he seemed, as the Wildings or the People of the Heights, or the lesser creatures of our valley, which fought and died for their own, yet were not cruel.

There came a day when his eyes opened and his own self looked out of them. Strangely, he asked few questions

of us, though he must have wondered much at his unlikely visitors, when the Wildings came shyly to his window to peep at their foundling. Much feeling had they for
this Perrin, for he came in company with a horse, which
they felt was one of their own kind, though far removed in
time from them. Yet they could communicate with the
creature in some odd fashion, and they brought to us
much broken and disjointed information which they had
gleaned from him.

This we patiently pieced together, forming a puzzling
picture which sent my mother into fits of white silence.

"War walks again in the outlands," she said to me. "The
forces which shaped Heraad and your father run like
wind in grass across the land. This poor beast was their
instrument; yonder gentle man was their victim. They
will seek to drive all under their whip or beneath the
earth. Such cannot tolerate that living beings may walk
free without their mark and brand. Now they harry their
own in their own place, but soon they will look afar—even
here, mayhap. So it has been among men for all of written
time, and it will not change for wishing it."

Then she was silent again, but I could see bitter memories etching their tracks across her brow, and I remembered what she had told me of my own father's senseless
cruelty. I shuddered as the edge of her cold anger
touched the hem of my thought. Then I hastened from
the room to see after our guest, fleeing that which so tor-
mented my mother.

I found Perrin trying to sit, that he might peer again
from the casement toward his grazing friend below the
window.

"It is good indeed that you feel so strong," I said, aiding him with pillows and propping him well. "Now you may look upon your friend at ease. How do you call him? Never did you speak his name in your delirium."

He frowned. "Truly, I have not named him. Some name he had, in his other life, and a master who treated him well; but when we came together, we were only two outcasts who suffered and needed a friend. Without his aid, I should have died in the grasslands. Without mine, I believe that he would have despaired and died of loneliness and his hurts." Then he smiled, and it lit his dark eyes with a pleasant glow and furrowed his lean cheek again into youthfulness. "I shall call him Friend, for such he has been to me."

Something there was in his look that made tears start to my eyes, and I turned to the window and called forth, "You have been named, good horse. Now you are Friend, and your master will soon be able to mount and ride forth to see our valley from your back."

As if he understood my words, the beast tossed his head and whickered, then trotted up to the window and poked his nose inside. Ears pricked forward, nostrils expanded, he looked inquiringly at Perrin, who sank among the pillows in a fit of laughter.

"She spoke truly, old friend. Do you doubt her word?" he choked to the horse, which bobbed his head solemnly up and down, as if nodding, then withdrew it and returned to his grass patch.

Then the contagion of laughter reached me, and I sat upon a stool and rocked with glee. Long we laughed, and when our peals had dimmed to hiccups, we smiled upon one another and were friends, for shared laughter is a sound bond between spirits. Even my mother, looking in to find the cause of such unbidden mirth, smiled, and some of the pain melted from behind her eyes.

"It is good to hear the bubbling of high spirits within these walls," she said. "Not since the time of my father's father has there been such company here. We have lived too soberly, I see, as though we were two grandams bearing the weight of years. I have let the old memories lie too heavily upon you, Cara, and upon me."

She took Perrin's hand, as she reached to lay her palm upon his forehead. "You have no fever today, youngling. Your hand is cool and steady. Soon you will be able to walk. But tonight, when Cara and I have done with our tasks, we shall make a fire against the spring chill, and then we will sit and tell tales and sing the old songs and make good cheer once again ring in the house. Now sleep, that you may be rested for it."

When he was settled again to rest, we went into the garden, for the spring was advancing and our young plants were striving vigorously with the encroaching grasses. Beneath the calm hand of the sun, we stooped and weeded and hoed, thinking, both of us, of the turmoil which stirred beyond our sheltering mountain. Though we never intruded upon one another with our seeking senses, still we knew when trouble sat within the heart. We felt the echoes of concern vibrating between us as we labored in the warm air, scented with crushed greenery and turning loam.

Balm for the spirit lay in our valley. Terror and death walked without. Yet we felt a pull within our hearts to turn our inward sight where we had never thought to send it, out into the world of men. Anger once again moved in our hearts, for such injustice as Perrin and his folk endured must awaken it in any who are just.

Yet we said no word, but labored together, leaving behind us straight rows of tidy lettuces and squash and beets. Whatever befall, from this patch of earth, and from the surrounding wood and meadows, came all our winter's provender, and, should we go forth again upon a stern errand, it must be left in good order, with a plea to the Wildings to see to its tending. But when the sun tilted far to westward, we straightened our cricked backs and looked, eye to eye, mind to mind. And we turned to the house and cleaned ourselves and made the evening meal and kept our word to our guest, laughing and singing and telling him of the doing of our fathers who lived on this spot.

Great interest had he. "Such folk have my own been, always, keeping their own ways and places and seeking no traffic with the bustle of the world. Warm have we been in things of the heart, rich in teaching and tenderness. To us, the step of the stranger has always meant suffering and flight, or death. So we have valued our home above all else—mayhap we have valued it too much, for the gods must remind us, at times, that we are as other men and subject to travail. Yet the hand of the tyrant will fall upon all, not solely upon errant Raithes, and their suffering will be worse than ours, I think, for they will not have been reared to resist, to persist, and to endure, as have we."

He fell back upon his pillow, a thoughtful crease between his brows. "I must recover my strength and return to my place, wherever that may now be," he said, tiredly. "Some of my folk still live—one I know certainly, and one I hold in hope. My people will need me, if they live. I must avenge them if they are also lost."

Tisha leaned forward and touched his wrist. "Hold no trouble in your heart, Perrin. Such will slow your mending. When you feel well and strong, then we will talk of your return. Mayhap"—she smiled—"you may go forth with companions who are not unskilled at war, though not of the sort that yonder tyrant knows. Be peaceful in spirit, for this will raise you to your feet long before you might otherwise stand."

Then she gestured to me, and I rose, saying, "Now we must all rest, for this day has been overlong and my eyes are closing as I stand. Good night to you, friend Perrin. May your dreams bear you into happier days again."

But when we reached the kitchen, we knew that our labors were not done, though we were weary to the bone. I went to the hearth and pulled the kettle into the coals. Tisha reached down the painted box that held our wild blackberry tea. We sat before the fire, relaxing, resting, drawing our spirits into focus, while the water purred to a bubble. The tea warmed us, inside to out, and we felt the weariness drain away, leaving our wits sharp and our inner eyes clear. Then we sat, side by side, upon the settle again and leaned our heads back upon the cushions.

Eyes closed, with the warmth of the firelight making a glow through our eyelids, we made our seeking senses into small projectiles, gathered, concentrated into utmost force and vigor. Together, these that were we moved across our familiar valley, speeding as never before, so

that Wilding and hart and Grack and all the other beings
and beasts were only a blur of sensing as we swept past.
Over the mountains we flew, feeling below us specks of
life of sorts we did not know; out onto the wide grasslands, now lit dimly by a new moon and a waning one.
Then we rose to a great height, feeling in a wide arc the
lands below us. Life there was, in abundance, but of
beasts. The sturdy bonfire of awareness that marks the
presence of our kind was not so near that we could feel it.

So we moved onward, toward the east, casting our nets
of seeking across all the world below. And we found men,
many of them, scattered into small groups, camped upon
the plains. We descended into the midst of such a group
and looked through the eyes of two of that company, feeling with their emotions. We recoiled at first, for they
were aboil with fear and anger and mindless panic. Yet
we persisted, and I saw about me a draggled lot of men,
fallen, most of them, into exhausted sleep. Those who
watched trembled at the stirring of the wind in the
grasses, the chirping of night birds, even the restless cries
of their own companions who dreamed ill.

The man whose self I sought to learn seemed more controlled, more master of himself. And truly, he was an officer, as I learned when the man who stood the watch
passed by and addressed him. Yet within his spirit there
was bitter fear and helpless anger and frustration. His
thoughts were closed to me, but such were his emotions
that I felt certain that those beings whom Perrin had
called Those Who Wait had been at work among all
his command, harrying, stampeding, harassing, creating
havoc among what had been a tautly disciplined army.

"Lord Tharan." A voice behind caused him to turn with spasmodic quickness, and I felt the flaring leap of his nerves, though his voice was almost calm when he spoke.

"Aye, Lushon?"

"Most of the men now sleep, Lord, but the horses are restless, and I misdoubt the picket ropes will hold them, should those demons begin to howl again. Yet I hate to rouse any of the men to watch them. Sleep is the only thing that may bring them back to themselves."

"True, old Sergeant. So we must let them sleep. I will go myself and double the tethering. That may hold. Keep watch, and call me from the lines should anything . . . untoward . . . come again."

The man called Lushon watched his commander walk into the darkness, and I turned my attention to him. But he was only a simple, frightened man, bound by habit and conscience to do as he was bidden. Yet he held a grim affection in his heart for that officer called Tharan, and I had felt no evil in him, for myself. He had seemed decent, perhaps reckless to a degree, but no wickedness walked in his heart. So I smiled at his sergeant's regard for him, and kept that officer in mind as Tisha and I rose to seek further.

All across those broad grasslands lay small pockets of men, most of them in exhausted slumber, nightmare-ridden. Some few there were who yet held themselves in control, but in the main man and horse alike existed in a state of shock and horror, twitching and moaning as they wandered in the fields of sleep.

Then we moved high in the air, my mother and I, and with one accord we sped through the deeps of the night toward Lirith, that city from which Tisha had fled in years long past. Without pause for remembering, she led straight to the tall house where sat the First Minister of Kyrannon.

Darkness filled that house; not only the blackness of night, but a murk that was a thing of the spirit. My questing sense almost recoiled, but I felt the presence of my mother beside me, and I followed that warm glow through the invisible halls and into a chamber where burned a faint light of the sort left for younglings who fear the dark. In that chamber slept a man, and he did not sleep well.

We looked down upon him, feeling for that which was the inner self of Him Who Sits at Lirith. And we found a well of unease, an uncertain and wavering creature shored up by the armor of his ambition. Within him there were walls hiding him from himself, doors leading nowhere, and a maze of self-deception fit to set one dizzy who sought to find the truth of that strange man. We turned from him, burdened with knowledge that sickened as it enlightened.

And as we turned to leave that house, he sat, suddenly, grasping the coverings of his couch to him, looking desperately about the room, as though he felt our presence.

"Who stands in my chamber?" he whispered. "Someone there is whom I can sense within these walls. Someone there is who has moved within my heart, as I dreamed ill dreams. Speak to me, that I may know I am not mad!"

Then, though we had never done before, Tisha and I forced our wills upon a new path, working upon the stuff of the air to form a whisper that came from no lips, formed by our thought. "We are retribution," we whispered. "Retribution," we repeated. And the words moved eerily about the room, swaying the hangings above the couch.

The tyrant sank upon his pillows, his eyes closed. He spoke in a normal voice, to himself. "I dream, still. No man walks without a body nor speaks without a mouth. And I have done no wrong to bring vengeance upon me. No guilt is mine, more than that of any powerful man who rules. I only dream."

He turned upon his side and slept again, so great was his power to deceive himself. Tisha and I returned from that place of sickness, through the streets, across the wide ways of Kyrannon to our own place, and we opened our eyes before our hearthfire, weary past words to say. The kettle still bubbled, and again we sipped tea. Then, stiff and sore as after a day of harvesting, we tiptoed to Perrin's door in order to see how he fared.

He slept deeply, and I looked upon his haggard young face and felt within myself a yearning warmth, a desire to aid and protect him. I looked at Tisha and she smiled a secret smile. Then we took ourselves to our rest.

Narrative of Tisha the Wise

Strange it is to waken to life, as from sleep, and to find that there still are tasks of import set before hand and spirit. Dreamlike has been my life, here with Cara in our hidden valley. Work and thought have sustained us, and our joys have been quiet ones; our tasks, until recent time, undramatic. But now the tide of the world has set in our direction, and we find ourselves readying for survival in those stormy seas that men call living.

For months, since the time when Heraad came and went, I have known unease. No seeking have I sent into the ways beyond the mountains, until now, for I wished not to know how the world fared. Knowing it unwise, I hoped, still, that we would be let to sink again into our dream, that never again would I be forced to sully my senses among the running sewers that are the spirits of so many who dwell outland. My Cara I had sought to shield from the knowledge that such folk live and walk in the clean winds of the gods. But such an one came: she learned within his heart of the ways our kind can seek, and it made her stronger than before, as I should have known it would. Even the wise can be foolish in the tending of their younglings.

Now Perrin sleeps at the end of the hall, bearing within

his wounded heart a chronicle of wrongs. Yet he holds no cankering hatred there, only a clean flame of anger. He seeks to set right what he can, which is the way of wise men far older than he. His pain permeates the house, like to the scent of blossom when the moon-trees bloom in spring, and I find myself weeping quietly as I go about my tasks.

Cara feels it more acutely. Not so well-versed in pain as I, she has yet to learn patience, and I sense her rebellious spirit's desire to be up and doing, her frustration at being unable to ease Perrin's agony. What can be done for his wounded flesh we are doing. But my poor child cannot yet see that his spirit must come through its crisis alone, and that only then will he mend and be a whole being capable of walking forth into battle again.

And I also know what she does not yet recognize. She will come to love him, as already he loves her. She cannot see the wistful glance he gives her retreating back, as I can. She cannot know his restlessness as he hears her step approach in the hall. In short, she does not know he loves her, for what does she know of love of man and woman? Such I could not teach her in words, for there are none shaped for it. In time she will come to know. With the help of the gods, there will be time, before he is well again, for them to come to terms with themselves and one another. And it is well that it should be so, for they are matched, like fine weapons. She is an arrow, far-reaching and penetrating. He is a sword, all force at arm's length. They will give me fine grandchildren.

But still I dream. It may be that none of us will survive the coming months, for, when Perrin is healed, we will all go overmountain into the world of Him Who Sits at Lirith, and that man will not allow us to live if it be within his power to slay us. For he will want us—desperately will he want us—in the vanguard of his armies, that they may walk unopposed over people shattered by our unfamiliar capacities. And when we will not serve him, he will know that he must destroy us or ever afterward live in fear. Would that we had the strength of spirit to slay him at such distance! Yet he also serves the gods and may not be destroyed without the opportunity to learn truth.

Only one day at a time need I live, I tell myself, quelling my own impatience. In their order and time, things will come to pass, and we must set about our work in earnest, that we may be ready. My own work is doubled—nay, tripled—for after the day's tasks are completed, I go to my couch and compose my body, then send my spirit questing forth. Once only have I taken Cara with me, that she might know what it is that we stand against. But she is young and has not come to her full strength. Such faring forth drains her more than she knows.

The years have seasoned me to toughness, so that my seeking afar is no such leaching away of strength. Into the mountains of the north have I gone, finding there three whom Perrin would rejoice to find. But I do not speak of them—yet. In the east is a lone woman, so like to Perrin in her heart that I know her for his sister. And she also is set about with horses. Strange it is how the beasts thread through this whole weft of happening, even our own Wildings being of that stock in far times. To the south rages one who bears a mixed burden of sorrow and hope. He is alone, and he has purpose within him which has subdued all other emotion. I seek to read him, but all I can discern is that burning purpose, which bears him on his way. He must be Perrin's kin, for he, also, is like. These Raithes bear within them a fiery spirit, distinctive to those who can feel such things.

These folk move in my perceptions, but there are also others whom I must find. For others there must be who are unwilling to bow the neck to Him Who Sits at Lirith, and in opposing such an one, it is well to have allies. So I must move over all the land of Kyrannon, in the places which I knew of old and the places where I never wandered, seeking for those who are angry and afraid and ready to lift their hands in the desperate wrath that is the hallmark of those who are not cowards.

While I search, our guest is healing, though more slowly than he would like. Upon waking, I went into his room and opened the draperies to the day. His wistful eyes sought out the distant form of Friend, cropping grass at the edge of the forest.

"When may I ride forth upon my horse?" he asked, as a small boy would, and I smiled.

"Before many weeks, I should think. When you can rise upon your legs without aid, turn quickly without feeling the earth spin beneath you, then you may mount yonder steed again. Patience, my child, will pay you well in this. For strength you will need, and more than strength, in the endeavor that lies before us. Let your body rest, let your spirit be tranquil, for a time. They have served you well in your battles thus far, and you must nurture them for future need. For now, take joy in being at ease, without need for starting at shadows and waking at sounds in the night."

Then Cara's hand touched the door-latch, and his whole attention fled toward her, leaving me to my thoughts, and to the work of the day. But I watched them as we tidied the room and set his morning meal before him, and my heart smiled, for they took pleasure in being together, in laughing, in the spillage of milk and the subsequent mopping up, in all the small things that make a life. Of such a comradely spirit is born a true marriage. But I must keep a cool face and a reserved mien, for too much approval from the old tends to set the young at odds with the wisest of fates.

Our tasks about the house completed, we took baskets and curved knives and set our feet upon the path into the forest, for the time was come to cut the buds and shoots which, with careful drying and storage, might be made into brews and ointments for healing purposes. The scented breeze of spring moved among the moon-trees, bearing the delicate scent of their blossoms abroad. The Grack moved, a glossy flash of busyness, among the branches, and we knew that his ravenous brood would halt his insatiable curiosity for a time. Yet, even in the midst of feeding his young, he found breath to send forth a strident "graaack!" that all in the forest might know we walked forth.

Down into the newborn greening of the forest we moved, with the straw-pale foliage of the moon-trees glowing above us like candle-flame. We left the nesting Grack behind, with his harried mate, and moved into the dells where dwell the Wildings. Finding the necessary saplings, we began trimming from them the parts needful for our medicines, but the peace that had lived always within the forest was there no more. A restlessness moved on the breeze, and we could feel the nervousness of the small creatures which hid all about us, burrowed in earth or nested in hollows.

"I feel," said Cara at last, "as though some magic spell had always protected this valley, and now it is withdrawn and we are exposed to the dangers of the world."

"It is true," I answered. "First outlanders entered, and their presence rippled widely across our place. Then we ventured outward, in spirit only, and in so doing we opened a passage for the unease overmountain to enter here. Feel you the Wildings about their tasks, quivering and ill-at-ease?"

We stilled to silence, feeling afar, through the deep places of the forest. Rasping across our seeking senses, there was tension; tension and fear rode the spring air. Then, cutting through the web of interlocking beings that was the wood, came a blast of emotion that shocked us from our feet, down into the ferny growths about us. We rolled onto our faces, gasping for ease, grappling with that elemental "I need!" that spoke from all the air.

Gladly would I have spared my child this terrible sensing, but she was caught, as was I, defenseless in the midst of practicing our art, and we were swept, in spirit, once again across the mountains, but not, this time, of our own volition. With a speed I had thought impossible, we were arrowed across the grasslands toward the northern mountains. Such was our velocity that, before we had adjusted ourselves to this strange happening enough to examine it, we were drawn down upon a great ridge of a mountain, into the forests that cloaked it to the summit, into a cavern that opened before us, and into the presence of two whom I, unknown to Cara, had been before, in my lone seeking.

But there had been three!

Narrative of Lengalyon

The power of need and the currents of power interact, at times, in ways so strange as to stagger the mind. So had the infant, whom Shanah has named Ashraf, called to me from the grasslands. So, now, have we called from afar to those with the potency to aid us.

Lulled by weeks of safety, Shanah, the child, and I lived quietly upon this height, taking care never to come into the open places upright, that any who might still seek might not learn of our presence. With my little garden and the bounty of the mountain to sustain us, we had no need to descend to the plains. Not so with our horses, who must graze more widely than the heights' limited grass patches. They must return to the lower places, we knew, in order to keep their strength against any great necessity for flight.

So we loosed them together, and they went away along the perilous trail, looking back, now and again, to nod their heads up and down as though assuring us of their speedy return, at need. And no doubt had either of us, for they were linked to us by more than love and stronger bonds than often bind man and beast.

Thus we felt little unease and passed the days with tasks and talk, always watching with awe the progress of the child. Ashraf grew as does any babe, sleeping much, eating greedily, but in his eyes was comprehension and often we felt the probing of his thought into ours, as though he read from the scrolls of our learning and experience in order to impress them upon his own new-minted mind. Almost it made us afraid, for no child of our race had ever been known to show such powers at so tender an age. Yet from him came no anger, no selfish "I want!" only searching curiosity and, I am certain, a wry amusement.

Attachment grew swiftly. I felt within him a spirit somewhat akin to that of my own lost son, but more than that bound us together. We felt spirit with spirit, that child and I, and knew one another more intimately than often happens among our kind. We found ourselves allied, as friends, incongruous as it seems in speaking of a graybeard and one so tiny that I could hold him in one hand. Yet we were united against a common foe, and both of us were aware of the fact.

As Shanah regained her strength and spirits, she began to range over the mountaintop, saying that she needed to stretch her muscles to full use again. But I knew that her heart cried out for her Raf, and her long rambles eased her against the pain which moved with her.

Yet I knew also that these wanderings abroad exposed her to risk, and I cautioned her against carelessness. Knowing Shanah as I now did, I felt secure in her judgment, and truly she was never overbold or less than wary. For long she measured her muscles against the slopes of the mountain, as if training for battle or far journeying. Her bow was busy, also, and she did not neglect sword and lance. But the gods were busy at their weaving of destiny, and all our care, all our precautions were overset, despite our efforts.

There came a day, not unlike those before it, when the child and I communed in the cavern, waiting for Shanah to return with game. We were relaxed, almost sleepy, and the sudden jolt of agony which burst from Ashraf caught me unprepared. Then I was pulled with him, in spirit, out across the mountain. And there upon the farther slopes we saw Shanah struggling in the hands of four men, who laughed grimly, until her sword drew blood from one, another. Then they overpowered her by their weight and strength and struck her senseless. As they turned to their horses, I saw the cause of her betrayal. Wandir, Plana, and Gollas stood in the edge of the forest, watching our enemies with a troubled air. Returning to us from their feeding, they had evidently been followed by a random band of troopers who had stumbled onto Shanah as she returned from her hunt.

Then the child and I were again in the cave, and his bruised spirit turned to me, searching for comfort. Knowing the forces which now confronted Shanah, I added my own force to his inner cry, and we sent it forth across the grasslands, seeking whoever could hear, until the land rang with our silent beseeching. We were answered strangely—most strangely—for there were with us in our place two who had not been there before. Almost we could see them, so strong were their presences.

But there was no necessity for seeing, or for hearing. They were with us and we with them, mind and spirit. All that we know, they also knew, and their knowledge was written upon our minds. Then we took counsel; the babe, the two women, and I. A strange assortment we were, but among us none led, none followed, for all were equal in capacities, though unlike. So it was laid upon the child and me to remain within our cavern, high on this mountain, but to range in spirit to find and gather together those of like heart with ourselves, giving them direction for their steps and guidance in their efforts.

"There is no distance too great for you to explore," said the spirit that was Tisha the Wise. "Across the Purple Waters there abide those who give their lives to wisdom, their hearts to truth, their hands to helping. Seek, if you can, the Initiates who dwell in the Towers of Truth. From them we may receive valuable aid."

"And do not fear for Shanah," added that spirit which was called Cara. "Her task is laid before her, and we must not seek to change it. But we can cheer her heart and send our strength through her hands, if there is need. Take comfort, Small One," and her spirit seemed to enfold the babe. "Your mother is in the service of the gods, and she is well able to work their will upon Him who Sits at Lirith. Surely she will return to you."

For a moment we were enwrapped, all four, in the warmth of our unity, the power of our purpose. Then they were gone, and only the babe and I sat in the cavern, looking within ourselves.

That night brought little rest for me, unused as I was to the full care of the child. My little goat, by good fortune, had freshened that spring, and milk there was in abundance for his hunger. But I felt unease and often waked and laid my hand upon him to learn if all was well.

Ashraf slept, but not with his usual wholehearted zest. There was within him an empty space that had been tenanted by his mother's physical presence, and his being was forlorn without her.

Morning brought the comfort of action. Both of us, I well knew, were anxious to begin our far-seeking, and I hastened with the morning tasks. When we were placed, he on his pallet, I sitting beside, ready for our casting, I paused and sent a query toward him. For a moment he considered; then agreement welled up in him.

Not in Kyrannon would we seek first. Better, it seemed to us, to find guidance for ourselves before hoping to guide others. And for that we must seek those who were far across the Purple Waters, away to the north and west of our continent. We first must find the Initiates.

Narrative of Raf dir Raithe

Strange are the ways of the gods. While those about me died, sword in hand, I found strength to keep my feet, and many were the dead men piled before me. But how the battle ended I cannot know, for I was struck senseless —from behind it must be—and knew no more until I came to myself long afterward.

It was dark—so dark that no shadow showed against it —and I swung, head down, feet down, crosswise upon a pack horse. I made no sound, but listened. For many heartbeats I heard only the creaking of leather and the soft thud of walking hooves. Then one who must have been riding with his stirrup near my head said, "There seems little need to go farther tonight, Nirac. Those who search the plains will be rounding up their quarry in the morning light, and it would be well if we waited and bore all prisoners to Lirith together. Then our lord may draw their secrets from them more readily."

"Aye, Horsemaster. It is in my mind that we passed a fair camping spot upon this road just a little onward toward Lirith. Mayhap five minutes will see us there."

Then again there was silence, and I gathered my wits as best might be and tested the thongs which bound my wrists. One who knew his work had tied them, and it would be no easy task to work them loose. More than five minutes—or perhaps five hours—I would need. So I ceased my twistings and pullings and hung as limp as a senseless man ought, waiting out my time with patience.

Well it was that I did, for when the camp-halt was made, I was swung from the horse and dropped untenderly beneath a bush, where a questing hand made certain that I was still well fastened, hand-to-hand and foot-to-foot. But none suspected that I had returned to my wits, and I did not open an eyelid or stir a muscle to inform them. Using the long training from my father and my marriage-kin, I relaxed from sole to scalp and rested while those about me settled noisily in for the remainder of the night.

I did not sleep. There was no need after my long unconsciousness. But now and again I smiled grimly, inside myself. For well I knew that none among these untutored troopers, not even their commander, dreamed what the morning would bring to them. I, being Raithe, could feel upon the wind the wrath of Those Who Wait, and I knew that their present business would soon be done, and that they would then turn their attention to all others of our enemies abroad upon the grasslands. Then there would be new work for me.

At last the campfires were doused and the sentries posted. The camp slowly sank into sleep. My hands busied themselves . . . one great twist to right, until the blood threatened to pop from the veins. One great twist to the left. Pause. Bracing heels of hands against one another, I strained against the thongs flatwise. Again and again and again. Long later, I knew that there was more slack than there had been. And by then the thongs were wet with blood, which relaxed their rigid texture a little.

Before dawn my hands were free. Long it seemed before I had flexed them into service, and even then they were swollen to bluntness. Yet they managed to free my feet, and I worked on in the darkness, seeking to return myself to usefulness.

Had I the management of the sentries, I should have slain all. No one of them came near me when watch changed, checking whether I were still secure. They were a slovenly crew, unused to discipline, and I used their own weakness to my advantage. I drew the thongs about myself to look as nearly undisturbed as could be done, that none who looked casually might see me free.

Then I waited, knowing that with the coming dawn terror moved down the wind upon the sleeping camp.

The first glimmer of light touched the east, and the sentries rattled their swords in the sheaths, signaling the others to wake. With mutters and groans, they rolled from their blankets and set about making their morning meal. The commander, yawning and bearded, was making his way leisurely toward my bush when the first cry moved upon the light breeze.

There was terror. There was anger. There was death in that cry, and all who heard knew. The horses snorted and reared in the picket lines, tearing loose stakes, tangling halter ropes, whinnying shrilly.

"'Ware the mounts!" the commander cried, and one who wore the cloak of a sergeant leaped to obey. But he was struck down by a pawing hoof, and no other stirred to aid him, all standing as though rooted in their places.

Then I laughed aloud and rose to my feet, seizing the sword from the commander's side.

"Haieeeeeeeee!" I cried, and the voices upon the grasslands came swiftly in answer, until it seemed as though the air were filled with vibrations that echoed inside the skull. Then the horses tore loose their impediments and ran away over the pasturelands, and the men sank to their knees, hands over ears, or else ran, too, in long, leaping bounds.

I stood alone, watching their flight, as the wave that was Those Who Wait swept about me, then past. Almost, I could see them. Almost, I could feel their touch as they swirled around me. Something inside my heart understood them, for with their passing I felt great peace of soul. Shanah lived, I knew, for they had told me. And our child also lived. And if my dear ones lived, then I might do great works upon the lands of Kyrannon.

Then I stepped across those who whimpered in my path, gathering what was needful for journeying. One horse, tied to a tree, had been unable to free himself, and stood, eyes rolled back into his head, ears flattened, teeth bared, listening to the horror in his spirit. Him I touched, speaking to him in the language we use to our own four-hooved children, and he calmed.

Leading him, I walked to the spot where the commander crouched, hands still over ears. I touched his knee with my boot-toe, and he looked up, at last, with glazed eyes.

"Tell Him Who Sits at Lirith," I said, and by the flicker in his gaze I knew that he attended, "that he has failed. The Raithe he most likely has slain, for he was old and would never run. Others of us fell, for I saw. But at least three live, and that is too many for his peace of mind. Tell him also that a Raithe dead is more fearsome than ten alive, and that he has multiplied the number of Those Who Wait upon the plains. Armies he has never dreamed of will rise against him. In the silence of the night," and here I spoke with a strange knowledge that came not from my own mind, "he will be attended by those whom he did not summon. Tell him that he has lost his gamble with the gods."

I turned and led the horse away into the road, mounted, and rode into the south, and did not look back upon that shattered troop.

Something there was in my heart that drew me southward, though I felt Shanah and the babe to be hidden to northward. Not south and east toward Lirith did I ride, but south and west, to the mountains which straddled the border between Kyrannon and Gryphos, which lay beyond. I felt myself to be an arrow, sent forth by the gods for their own purposes, and willingly I went. Somewhere, there in the shadowy passes and forested peaks, lay my task; and I hastened, spurred by the anger which simmered ever beneath my present thought.

Not one of the Raithes gifted with the long vision had I been, in the past—perhaps because there had never been great need for that ability. Yet my spirit seemed to seek abroad for hearts like unto my own, for spirits filled with anger and dread. And as I journeyed, day following day, I grew certain of my goal. No thought did I catch, nor glimpse from other eyes, but I felt despairing hatred ris-

ing before me from the mountainous ways, and I knew
that I must seek there.

A week's journey saw me folded into the arms of the
mountains. Then I went warily, for I hunted for desperate
souls who would not know me to be at one with their purposes. As I followed the looping trails that wound higher
and higher into the forests, I made certain that my sword
was sheathed and the sheath hidden among my blankets,
my hands well in the open, my face raised that any who
watched might see my features.

And I was watched. That newly wakened sense within
felt the weight of hidden eyes upon me. Even my mount
paced cautiously, ears pricked, as if he were as uneasy as
I. Yet there nothing for it but to continue our way up the
narrow path, with sheer drop to a stream to left and steep
slope upward to right. No view had we of any save a
short portion of the way, for it switched back and forward, gaining the height. We were blind and helpless,
should any think to attack us, yet I felt the pull of fate
and the will of the gods within me, and we went on.

Long it seemed before we reached the top, where the
path leveled off to wind among great pines. There lay a
flat space, bare to the rock, edged with grass-patches, and
there I stopped and dismounted, easing my horse after his
efforts. As he cropped the grasses, I stood forth in the
open space and looked about me. Though I could see no
living soul, I said, "You who watch, come forth. No
enemy am I to you, only to Him Who Sits at Lirith.

"Two days and seven agone, I sat within the home of
my marriage-kin, preparing for battle. None had we
offended, none had wo injured. By living in freedom, with

our great horses, we had attracted his notice and his avarice, and we knew that his troops would come upon us
soon. Nine of us there were, and we fought as best we
could against ten times our number. The fates of my wife
and my kin I cannot tell, for I was struck senseless and
captured. Yet I came forth from the hands of the horse-
guard and the gods have sent me hitherward, searching
for those who have also cause to fear the attentions of the
Tyrant. Come forth, for my sword is not at hand."

There was long silence, marked by a distant birdcall. I
closed my eyes and willed them to feel what was in my
heart, holding breath and forcing the thought so strongly
that my temples pounded.

When I opened my eyes, a man stood atop the stony
outcrop before me. No sound did he make, no word
moved between us as he stood considering me with
strangely light-hued eyes set in a broad face lined with
the scars of battle and the scars of time. After a space, he
spoke.

"What house sends you forth, and what family?" he
asked in a voice that rumbled through his barrel chest
and came forth as subdued thunder.

"I am kin and marriage-kin of the old house of Fallowden, far to north on the grasslands. Raithe am I, and
Raithe my wife, and our folk are herders of fine horses
and have been for many lives of men."

He grunted. "Somewhat I know of the old Raithe. Not
always have I perched upon a crag in these cold heights.
I held a Fallowden horse once, long years ago. Before its
owner would make trade with me, he sent me across the
plains to a meeting with the Raithe, that he might judge

my fitness to handle one of his beasts. Old he was, even
then, and came thundering up to our meeting-place upon
a great stallion that moved with the wind in his teeth."
He grunted again, then leaped lightly down from his hiding place.

He walked to my horse and regarded him from all
sides. "No Fallowden steed, this," he said at last.

"We left none where the toads of the Tyrant might find
them," I said in reply. "This poor beast I took from my
captors, when I left them."

He grinned, and his eyes squinted shrewdly. "So easily
is it done, nowadays? You just take horse and away, without halt nor thank-you?"

"I . . . had some aid," I said, wondering how much
should be entrusted to him concerning the stranger ways
of my people.

"Oho!" he shot back. "So strange voices still call upon
the plains, do they? Well can I understand that those who
serve Him Who Sits at Lirith might run mad at their cry.
Come now with me, Raithe of Fallowden. We shall go to
seek the Lord Thonar, who holds the peace in his hand—
though little enough peace have we seen for many
weeks."

So we went forward on the path, he waiting with cautious politeness for me to go first, leading my steed. And
my heart was almost at ease, for I felt my task now within
my grasp and was no longer driven toward its discovery.

Narrative of Doshan the Hammer-Hand

Never did I think, in my restless youth, to squat behind a rock upon a mountain, awaiting attack by the lawful ruler of my country. Strange are the twists of fate that tangle the feet of the unwitting walker in the world's paths. So I watch upon the height, and the years of training that were my birthright as a soldier's son are turned against the powers that honed me to be a blade in their defense.

For months before I fled from Lirith, I had known that trouble was in the wind. From my post as Sergeant of the South Gate I saw strange messengers go forth and return along the road that leads, beyond the swamps at river-mouth, to Gryphos. Troops jangled forth on short forays and returned with wild-eyed farmers to be trained under duress as pikemen and archers. In the barracks, in the taverns, there was talk among the soldiery and the commoners—always talk, and that always of coming war.

War held no fear for me, who had been sent afar with armies-in-training to aid the brother of the old King of Kyrannon, now long dead, in his wars with invading barbarians, who came across barrens to attack his rich city. One who survived those years of waking at night with painted madmen swarming in the torchlight, of blade-to-blade struggles knee-deep in thornbrush, of festering wounds and constant gut-sickness—such a one, in short, as I and a few others from the old days, found little excitement and less pleasure in the growing buzz of war-gossip. But we were soldiers, and such was our business, so we did not dread whatever was to come.

Yet neither did it sit well within my craw that what drew near came at the behest of the new First Minister. Something I knew of him, for in his youth he had ever edged about the haunts of the troops. Though he said little, there was that in his eyes that told me he missed nothing and surmised much. At first I thought him one smitten with the life of the military, but I soon discarded the notion. There was something far too calculating about him, far too knowing and sly.

No word did I hear of him, then, for years, as we grew older, I to late middle age, he to mature years. But I was not astonished when, amid the turmoil attending the death of the old Minister, he stepped forth, at last, with the seal of office in his hand. For there were officers in my own troop who had spoken, in unguarded moments, of one in a high place who dealt generously with them, offering them his regard—nay, his friendship, indeed. I had wondered if that one might not be the fox-eyed one whom I remembered with a shiver in my soul.

So it was indeed. He had made his discreet purchases wisely for his purposes, choosing those in a position to make easy his passage into the seat of power. But he did not know that one there was who had eye upon him. Aye, and that was I, watching from the comfort of obscurity the fates of those whom he had chosen to lever him to the heights. First one, then another of those overawed men found exile, or death, or unexplained disappearance their destiny. And still I watched and listened, in tavern and alley, at the gates and in the city. All that I learned I recorded, naming the sources of the tales I heard, if I could ferret them out.

A picture formed that was no flattering one. The new First Minister of Kyrannon found no deed beneath his abilities, no subtlety of dishonor outside the reach of his capacities. The more I probed beneath the seeming of the man, the greater the stench I stirred.

At last I found it too much to bear alone. It came into my heart that could I but place my findings before the eyes of those who wielded power in Lirith, they would be forced by their own consciences to remove such a man from the place which he had stolen. So I, in my graybeard innocence, sent a message to the foremost merchant in Lirith, who had the name of an honorable man. Not so unwary was I that I stated my case therewith, but I implied more than was wise—as I learned to my cost.

For messenger, I chose a youngling who served as orderly to My Lord Renvah, who commanded my troop. The child had been kicked and beaten until his senses nearly left him, when first I knew him, as a result of his making a trifling error in the ordering of the Lord Renvah's boot-polish. I am not one for coddling the young, but him I nursed back to wholeness, and I knew that he held an attachment for me that would keep his tongue still.

Well it was that I chose him, for he returned with pale face and shaking limbs.

"You must go, Doshan, and quickly," he told me as he

entered my doorway. "Your message I delivered safely, but something within me kept me loitering in the way beside yon merchant's house. Not ten minutes passed before the servant who took the message came out in great haste. I followed him, and he went to the house of the First Minister and hammered upon the door. There was much to-do before the Minister himself came out into the way and closed the door behind him, as though to speak privately. I heard your name, and the Minister said, 'Arrest him!' and I slipped away and ran to warn you. Hurry!"

I did not wait to question the lad, but warned him to seek his own chamber and to know nothing, if asked. Then I took up my pack, which was always ready for unexpected faring-forth, and went out into the hallway. As I sped down the broad stair, I could hear boot heels in the paved square without. Then I knew that I must fight and run. But not for mere fancy have I ever been nicknamed the Hammer-Hand. The seal of my fist has been set upon many a man, in my long years of soldiering, and my fists I would use, but never a sword against those who had served with me.

So I burst into the midst of the arriving men, suddenly as a whirlwind, and many a head rang against my fists as I swept through the confused group. Then I was clear of them, running to scale the wall. A leap and a scrabble took me over, and I slid into the shadows of the twisting ways of the city and knew that none might find me there.

A recessed doorway gave me shelter as I removed my soldier's garb and donned the wide-legged trousers and pointed jerkin of a horse-handler. The long-tasseled cap came well down over my ears and I wrapped the long tail of it around my neck, as if against the night-chill. Rolling my old garments into a tight wad, I dropped them into the flow-drain of a fountain at the corner, then I shouldered my pack and turned into a cross-street.

Plodding wearily, as though I had been walking for long, I turned my steps toward the Soldiers' Compound. It was not long before I heard hurrying feet, and a part of my pursuers came into view, peering into doorways and over garden walls as they approached. As they drew near, I halted and asked, "What news, sirs? Whom do you seek, so late?"

The officer motioned to the man with the lamp, and he raised it high. The gods were with me, for none were men whom I knew.

"We seek a criminal, dressed as a sergeant. Has no one passed you, fleeing as for his life?" he asked.

"No man have I seen for some time," I answered, scratching my ear beneath the bulge of the cap. "And none at all coming from yonder," and I nodded toward the Compound.

He grunted disgustedly, then cried an order. The group wheeled into a side street and were lost to my view. I grinned into the darkness and sauntered on, whistling a dreary teamster's trail-song. Before light touched the east I had left the city behind, leaving no guard at any gate the wiser; for none know the boltholes from the city as do the Sergeants of the Gates, who must stop them in time of peril.

So I came, along the south road, to the great river-swamp which marks a part of the boundary of Gryphos. Then I turned west, following the river into the mountains which rise higher and higher, the farther into the west one travels.

I had known that troops rode this way. I had not realized the aim of all their expeditions, and though I expected the families of abducted farmers to be wary I felt safe in my unmilitary clothing. But I had not known of the bright metal mined in the mountains, nor of the fiercely free people who brought it from the depths into the light and smelted the ore. And I knew nothing of Lord Thonar, who ruled there with light hand and wise heart.

But I learned. As I worked my way into the heights, following road and path and trail, I felt myself watched, though no watcher could I see. When I reached the point which it is now my task to watch, I paused and wiped my brow. Then there came a voice, soft as midnight birdcall, yet stern as the sword at my side.

"Halt, traveler," it said. And such was the tone that one could see, deep in his heart, the drawn bow and the nocked arrow that enforced that demand. "Lay aside your pack and stand forth unarmed."

So I did, stepping into the center of the stony clearing, hands spread wide that any might see them empty. Then my captor stepped forth, also, from behind the rock, and she held the bow half-drawn. No soft woman of the city was this, and I knew that she held my death in her hands, should I move unwarily. So I stood, awaiting her orders.

Thus it was that I went before Lord Thonar as a prisoner, taken by one whom I could have snapped between thumb and forefinger. Yet this did not rankle as it might have, for within the hidden village all went armed and no task seemed set aside for men or for women. None jeered at me as I was taken past, toward a great outcrop of stone that towered above the cup where the settlement lay.

Then I forgot all such vain musings, for my captor directed me through a maze of rockfalls which were traps for the unwary. And at the end of that rough path there was a sharp and narrow angle which led into an arched opening in the face of the rock. One archer from above— one swordsman just past the bend—could have held the place against all the army of Kyrannon, and I saluted the Lord who had chosen such a place for his keep.

There were no servants within, though folk hurried about as though they attended many tasks. But no seneschal ushered us into a state chamber and no fawning footman opened great doors. Then the woman with the bow spoke, for only the second time in our brief acquaintance.

"My Lord Thonar, I bring one who walked the mountain. He stood at my command, and he has shown no desire to flee." Thus and no more she spoke, and I marveled, for each time in my life that I have thought to marry, the gabble that it involved sent me flying.

The Lord Thonar was sitting at a desk in a small chamber and looked to be reckoning accounts. He raised his head and smiled at my companion, which caused his many wrinkles to seem to dance about in the flickering torchlight of the room.

"Well done, Tathira. We shall winnow the truth from him. Mayhap he will come to be one with us. Thank you, my child."

She raised her hand in a half-salute and was gone without sound of footfall.

Though I should have been attending my host, I looked after her. "None such did I ever meet in the lowlands, else I should not be now unwed," I said, half to myself, making a resolve in my heart that only Tathira could bring to fruition.

Then Thonar laughed, a great rich chuckle that shook him in his chair. "No spy ever bore himself so, I'll warrant. Let us search now for the truth of ourselves. I am Thonar, by the grace of these folk, their lord. Since Kyrannon has been, my people have mined the metal from these heights and worked the ore into bright stuff for sword and armor, for pot and plow. Free are we all, and have ever been. No ruler who ever sat at Lirith has claimed any rights over us nor sought more of our metal than he was willing to barter for in fair trade. So we have lived in our own way for many lives of men, and so we will live until our ends. We are not warriors, but we are strong and determined, and none sent against us by Him Who Sits at Lirith shall return unharmed to their master."

"Troops have come against you?" I asked, stunned, for never had I known that the rulers of Kyrannon had sent armed might against their own folk.

"Aye," said the old man, and his face was suddenly grim. "Troops came, as far as they knew to come, and they called out our sentries and bade them fetch me. Arrogance such as this angered my folk beyond endurance, but I held them to silence and I came. And the fools handed to me a proclamation which declared us all to be slaves of the First Minister, bound to deliver to him all stores of metal now worked and to meet quotas at intervals for all future time.

"Then I struggled mightily with my own spirit, for I desired nothing so much as to smite dead the ignorant young fool who presented me with this insult. Yet I seemed mild as milk, saying 'Aye, sir,' and 'Nay, sir,' and putting them off with tales of the great task it would be to bring all our worked metal to the lowlands for their awkward carts to transport. So I gained a month. And at its end, we had a fair pile of metal for their taking, which satisfied them, for they know nothing of us and our works. Then we knew ourselves safe from interruption until the time set for the quota-gathering, and that time is three months away.

"Now tell me your tale, for you have the look of a man with something to say."

I drew a long breath. "I have been a soldier of Kyrannon for all of my days, and my father and grandsir before me. No thought had I ever known that was disloyal to my country. Yet when the present First Minister seized power, I was dismayed, for somewhat I had observed of him, in his youth, and my soul mistrusted him.

"There were those who revealed, in my hearing, that he had favored them, and they were those who held places near to the seat of power. So I watched, and this is what I learned." And I went to my pack, which Tathira had dropped beside the doorway, and I drew forth the packet which I had prepared for the eyes of that merchant in Lirith."

Those papers were my passport to the mountain keep, for when the Lord Thonar had read them he extended his hand to me in friendship and offered me the ordering of his unformed army. And do not think him uncautious for thus giving a stranger his trust. He was a man unblinded by fear or caution, though he was cautious. His own assessment of a man was his yardstick, and this he trusted.

So it came about that I was the one who squatted behind the rock at trailhead when Raf dir Raithe came up the mountain. And as my wife and I conducted him to the keep, we questioned him, for I am not as closemouthed as Tathira, as she often now reminds me. We found him pleasant, even friendly, but cautious. And I felt in him a bottled-up rage that all but lit his dark face from within, like to a lantern.

Something there was about him that reminded me of Thonar; some cast of feature, manner of moving. But a Thonar full of youth and pain and anger. And purpose.

As we approached the keep I noted his eyes moving from point to point, noting guardposts, assessing its impregnability. Small nods punctuated each of his observations, and his face grew less tense, his posture less wary.

"One who thinks much has made this aerie," he said as we went into the maze. "No fighter could ask for better ground to defend."

Then he raised his head and smiled and led me through the maze as though he had walked it each day of his life. Tathira slipped ahead to rap upon the door, that Thonar might be warned of our approach, but as she lifted her hand the panel moved, and Thonar stood before us, gazing upon our captive with excitement in his eyes.

"I give you greeting, Brother," he said, and the newcomer stepped swiftly forward and took his hand.

"I come with the aid of the gods, Kinsman," he said.

We stared, Tathira and I, as the two embraced as do relations who have been long parted.

"Come into the chamber of accounts and sit, my friends," said Thonar, turning to my wife and to me. "This is a strange happening, and you must find, with me, what purposes the gods hold in heart for us."

So we went in and sat, dazed and wondering. And the young man stood before us and said, "No thought had I, in my long journey from the grasslands, that the gods were guiding me toward one who shares the blood of my family. For you, My Lord," he said, nodding toward Thonar, "are Raithe, as I can tell in my bone and heart. Yours was the spirit that cried to me from afar, in rage and sorrow, drawing me hither. Is it not true?"

"Aye," said Thonar slowly. "My mother was even such as you, tall, slender, darkling-wise, and strong as sword-blade. She, too, felt afar with her inner self, and my father was guided by her visions. We knew that she came from the grasslands upon a steed like no other, seeking for my father, who had need of just such as she. They were joined, as steel and magnet, for their lives' length, and he outlived her by less than a day. Nolathe ni Raithe was the name we carved upon her tomb."

"So," said the dark man. "And you may call me Raf dir Raithe, who wedded Shanah ni Raithe of the house of Fallowden."

I started and interrupted, "Aye, and kin to the old Raithe of that house. Might your mother have been sister-kin to that wise one?"

Raf nodded slowly. "The Raithe was only one of many children of his father. In his youth terror descended upon

Fallowden, as it had before and has since done, and they scattered as straws before the whirlwind. None save he and his wife found their way again to the hall of their people. I have not heard named all those who were lost or slain in that time, but, as time goes, it might have been his sister who rode here to make her life anew."

"Strange are the ways of the gods," said Thonar, turning to fold his hands upon his writing table. "But we have our own tasks to perform in their behalf. Let us take counsel among ourselves and seek wisdom."

Then we heard the tale of the rape of Fallowden, so far as it was known to our guest, and the account of his escape from the horse-guard of the Tyrant.

"Thus I was sent to you, and for a purpose. We must hold our hearts in patience until that purpose is revealed to us, but I feel within my spirit the motions of strange powers, winging abroad over the lands about, and I feel that we shall be counseled by wiser than we, before the day of reckoning comes for Him Who Sits at Lirith." So spoke Raf, and we nodded, Tathira and I, for somewhat do we know of the intricate weft which the gods can shape upon the loom of fate.

So we arm ourselves, laboring long in the mines and at the smelters, clanging at the forges and shaping weapons against the needs of the future. The twang of bow and the clatter of swordplay may be heard about the height, as we train the people to wield them artfully. No bird flies across the skies unmarked; no chipmunk scurries up our paths unwatched.

We wait upon the gods, but they shall not find us weak and unprepared.

Narrative of Kla-Noh the Initiate

Many are the heart-cries heard in the Tower of Truth, calling afar in time of grief or danger, seeking aid from those wiser and more knowing than the common run of men. Most often, those pleas are moved to us upon the power of the Shamal, that crystal of potency which we make by our arts, that those afar may speak with us.

Yet, once in long spans of time, we may find ourselves caught in a beam of purest sending, spirit to spirit, across terrible distances. Then we focus our alertness, for urgent need is winged upon such calls.

Thus it was that I waked, deep in the night, to a pulse of summoning that shattered my dream and brought me upright within a heartbeat. No crystal-focused message was this, for such come as voices. This was a wrench at my heart, a pulling at my spirit, a probing into my thought itself. It enwrapped me, fogging my senses for a moment, as I put my robe about me and set off through the Tower to the chamber of Ru-Anh, the Father of Initiates.

Age has set its seal upon me: I forgot my slippers, and my feet burned coldly upon the stone flags as I hurried, and I smiled to think upon the astonishment of Ru-Anh when he awoke to find me at his bedside in such case.

Even the bone-ache which traveled from joint to bone to ligament served only to hurry me on. Not since the old days, when I sought after secrets in the streets of Shar-Nuhn, had I known such excitement as I now felt. I had thought my wild adventures finished when I entered the Tower, but I felt in my innermost self that my most difficult task might still lie before me.

Ru-Anh woke to my touch upon his shoulder, completely, as always.

"Kla-Noh, my brother-in-thought, you come to me late —or early! What brings you from the fields of sleep to my door?" he said, pulling on his tunic and endeavoring to settle his beard comfortably over the top of it.

"A call such as I have never felt before," I answered. "Open your senses wide to the winds of the gods. You will hear it within you."

"Little need have I for that," he answered. "The pulse of that thought beats upon me, now that I have waked. Let us seek out Nu-Rea, for she is most able, among us all, to deal with this cry in the night."

Then we hurried away down the passage and up the stair, our beards fluttering behind our shoulders with the speed of our haste. Yet, though I felt urgency, I felt no impending tragedy, only interest that was quickening to intensity within me, interest and a strange desire to laugh aloud at the picture we made as we moved through the silent Tower.

Nu-Rea slept in a shielded keep, deep in the Tower. So sensitive was her spirit to the joys and despairs of others that she could not survive for long when unprotected from the constant washing away at her heart of the sea of emotion that troubles all men. Her door was of heavy wood faced with brazen plates, and to knock upon it was unavailing. We pulled upon the cord that rang the bell in her chamber. Then we stood, waiting upon the chill flags for her to waken.

The cold had taken possession of my toes, and I contrived to stand upon one foot, warming the other on the top of the first. Ru-Anh looked at me strangely, for a moment, seeking the cause of my storklike attitude. Then he reached into the recesses of his outer robe and drew forth a pair of felted bedsocks.

"I cannot allow one of our order to freeze by inches," he said gravely. "It ill befits those of our age and dignity to hop about barefoot in the night." His eyes twinkled as though he, too, felt the wild desire to burst into laughter.

As I clothed my colder foot, the door swung open and Nu-Rea stood before us. She showed no surprise, for well used was she to being summoned at strange hours upon stranger missions.

"Let us go up, my child, into the Seeking Chamber," said Ru-Anh. "There is a strange call lying upon the heart, this night."

She nodded. "Through my shielded walls I have felt it," she said. "I was donning my robe when you pulled upon my bell-rope. But this is a strange cry that calls us from sleep—I feel within it many emotions, and I often wish to laugh aloud."

Now we were three who hurried through the halls, but as we passed doors, many opened, and when we reached the Chamber almost half our complement stood behind us. Without words, for there is little need for spoken instructions among the Initiates, we took our places in the deep chairs that circled the room. Hand linked to hand, as our heads went back against the cushioned rests until we formed a circle of mind and strength, all focused upon Nu-Rea, who sat in a tall chair before a table where lay a complex of crystal and cobweb-fine silver wire.

At the center of the tool which was upon the table burned a great Shamal, its amber fires pulsing with light, almost angrily, though we knew that no like crystal was attuned to it in this calling. Yet this, the Mother of the Shamals, was alive with the strength of the caller, and Nu-Rea leaned forward and placed her hands upon the crystal's faceted upper face. Those who sat upon either side laid their hands upon her shoulders, and with that connection we made contact with those who sought us from afar.

And we laughed. With astonishment and a strange joy, we laughed, for we found that we had been called from our beds by a sending of terrible strength and purpose—hurled upon us by one of graybeard years and a tiny babe. Clearly could we see them, within our spirits, sitting in a cavernlike place before a fire, the babe held in the curve of the man's arm, eyes closed, sending their spirits forth to find us.

The voice of the man spoke within us, and we listened eagerly, for in all the time we knew, never had there been so strange a seeker after our aid. A long tale he told us, of tyranny and battle and death—and life. Upon the continent far to the south and east of the Purple Waters he sat, and the leagues were as nothing, for his thought was reinforced by the spirit of that strange infant, who lay quietly upon his arm, listening with his heart to our communication.

Truly they had need of us, for within that land, which they called Kyrannon, walked folk who held up the hands of the gods. But they were few, and they faced a tyrant armed with all the weapons of the world. Yet, scattered though they seemed to be to our friend Lengalyon's best knowledge, they were following, each in his lonely way, the paths laid out for them upon the map of time.

"We—the child and I—sit upon a mountain, helpless to aid with hand or blade. Only with our spirits may we bring succor to those who walk afar. Tisha, that wise woman, directed us toward you for advice and added strength, so we sought across the ways of the wind for answering spirits, and you have spoken to us. But without the child I could not have reached to such distances after you. There dwells within his small frame a power so great that it seems almost frightening. Seek you within him, that you may know the true source of this sending." So spoke Lengalyon.

Then we turned our hearts toward the small one, and surely there blazed from him, in response, a flow of emotion which spoke to us as well as words. Grief there was, for the loss of his mother from his side. Anger there was, though he did not clearly understand its source. Love there was, for his companion. And, rippling over all as light across running water, there was laughter. He could see us, as we could see him, in the mirror of his thought, and he found us humorous. And, seeing the reflection of ourselves through his untaught senses, we also laughed to see the circle of blue-robed figures sitting solemnly about a room, eyes closed, hands clasped together.

Again we laughed, at ourselves, and with that shared joy we felt that young spirit link with us, forming bonds stronger than any formed by flesh. Few of our number have known the presence of children, though some there are who came late to the Tower after their worldly tasks were done. Yet, to all of us, that small spirit spoke with the most innocent joy, and we responded. So the linking between us, though across so great a distance, was made smooth and sure, and we knew that, at need, they could seek our further aid.

Nu-Rea now leaned toward the Shamal and spoke into it, amplifying her voice and our thoughts with its aid. "Little do we know of warfare and battle," she said, echoing the sum of our spirits. "Yet we may strengthen the hands and the hearts of those who must stand before the enemies of the gods. We are at the side of every man or woman who takes the work of the gods in hand. For this purpose have we been taught and nurtured in wisdom. One there will be who watches, with your aid, those who do battle in Kyrannon. And when the time is ripened, all the strength of our spirits will pour into those who have need of it. This we promise."

The eyes of the seekers opened, and we felt that their hearts were comforted by her words. "One of us will be ever alert and ready to call for you, when necessity beckons," said Lengalyon. Then the pulse dimmed as a mist dissolves in a breeze, and we saw and felt them no longer.

Nu-Rea sank back into her tall chair, her head dropping back to rest against its cushion. "There will be need for one to attune himself for this call."

Then I stood and said, "This, I feel, is a task set me by the gods. I shall be the link, if it be the will of the Order."

So I wait, as I go about my tasks and my studies, to join once again with Lengalyon and that marvelous babe, forming a channel for the power that flows between those who will only good.

Narrative of Perrin dir Raithe

There came a day when I mounted Friend and rode across this valley, from the moon-tree wood where dwell Cara and her mother to the forest-edge, past the Wilding dells, where the stony mountains begin their march upward. Once again I bore myself as a man and no sickling, bound to his couch. Yet those weeks of my healing had been dear ones to me, smoothing away hurts from my spirit, as from my flesh.

As I turned to look back at the stone house where I had lain so long, I saw my two friends stooping in their garden, hands moving among the plants. Cara looked up, as though feeling my gaze, and lifted her hand. Then joy shot through me, and I rode forward, singing within myself, though no seemly melody has ever passed my lips.

It is beyond my poor skill to tell of the pleasure I held in my wanderings, for I had been within walls for longer than ever in my life before. Friend bore me where he would, for all places were strange and delightful alike, and we went first to the Wilding dells.

They greeted me with their shy dignity, and they welcomed Friend as one of their own. More than one, when I took my leave, laid his hand upon mine and said, "When need calls, we are here," and I felt that this must be a great concession from these peace-loving folk.

With the westering of the sun, I turned back toward home—and I knew that, happen what might, my home would be where Cara dwelt, be it here or elsewhere.

Through the moon-trees I rode, feeling the peace inside myself. But a sudden harsh "Graaack!" above my head woke me from my ease, and I looked up to see a shiny black bird watching me with much interest. Then, far down the path toward Tisha's home, I heard another such cry, and another, and another. Soon I heard flying feet, and Cara came into my view, running lightly to meet me. Her eyes were alight with excitement, and I knew that now was the time when matters moved abroad, drawing us back into the world of tyranny and death which I had fled.

Friend halted without my touch upon the rein, and Cara, without slowing, swung herself up behind me. At her touch I felt tears rise in my eyes, and I did not look around, that she might not see, but only touched the horse's flank with my heel.

"Where away, my Lady?" I asked, when I could trust my voice.

"Things happen overmountain!" she cried. "We must ride home with all haste, for there is need of our strength and knowledge."

"But I have no gift of spirit," I said. "How may I aid in this, which will move your thought where I may not follow?"

"You are Raithe," she said, and I could hear a smile in her voice. "There are powers in your blood that you have not used or known. And you are near in heart to those whom we must bespeak. Also," and her hand patted my shoulder lightly, "you are healed of your wounds and may lend us your strength, that we may do our work well and completely. Never think that we will not need you in this undertaking."

Tisha stood before the house, glimmering among the moon-trees in her gray robe as though she might be a wraith. But her face was afire with purpose, and her eyes struck sparks of excitement in my heart. She laid her hand on the rein and loosed the bit as we halted before her.

"Friend," she said to the horse, "you may rest and graze for now, but we will soon need your patient back to bear us away over the mountains. Go and take your ease." She struck him gently on the rump, and he looked back to see that we were safely dismounted before he whickered and moved away to his grass-patch.

Then she turned to me and took my hands. "Perrin, we must begin our labors. Today we must send our spirits abroad to find your kin who are scattered widely across the land. For this we need you—your knowledge of them, your love for them will give us a lodestone to guide us rightly. We must give them direction, that their efforts may mesh with ours—and those of others who also labor in this field. So few are we who stand fast before the Tyrant that we cannot afford the waste of any. Come now, and we will eat and drink and sit at rest, building our energies for the task."

I bowed my head, and she kissed my forehead. Then we went into the house, leaving the summer dusk to fade, as we lit the lamps and built up the smoldering fire that burned ever on the kitchen hearth.

Our meal was a merry one. It seemed that we had all

been waked from a foreboding dream, and now that the time of action was come we were light of heart. Even my slow tongue turned many a jest, and we laughed among ourselves as innocently as children, though we knew that as the darkness fell without, so did darkness of another sort fall upon all Kyrannon.

When we were done and had made all tidy within the house, then we sat upon the settle before the hearth with cups of the aromatic tea which Tisha brewed from berry leaves. A drowsy peace descended upon us—almost a sleepiness—as we gazed into the red coals. Tisha sat upon my left and Cara on my right, and after a time I took Cara's hand in my own. She did not move it nor frown, but turned and looked deeply into my eyes. Then she smiled, and there flowed between us another bond than that of friendship. Without the gift of soul-searching though I believed myself to be, yet I knew what passed within her as within myself, and we sat in warm contentment.

Tisha stirred at last. "My children," she said, "you have made your bond, and I am well pleased. But now it is time for us to take our strength in our hands and to go outward toward our long task. Lay aside your cups and join hands, all three."

This was done in a moment.

"Now, Perrin, think upon your sister Ruthella. She dwells, I am convinced, in a valley in a fold of mountain or hills, surrounded by horses. One such have I found, as I sent my spirit abroad, and she seemed so like to you that I knew her for Raithe. Think of her, who must be Ruthella, for Shanah is elsewhere."

I started. "You have found Shanah? And the child . . . did it live?"

Tisha tightened her grip on my hand. "Both live and are well, though Shanah goes into danger. For this reason we are moving so soon. We must send all aid for her. And the child thrives in good care and will make all of his blood awe-stricken, ere he stands upon his feet to walk. Now think of Ruthella."

So I closed my eyes and thought of my sister. So quiet a girl, yet one who laughed often. Patient to deal with all our strange family, happy in her love for Millis—and what of Millis? He did not survive, I think. But I drew my thought from this false trail and set it again upon Ruthella. If she were among horses, then she had gone east, to the secret horse-pastures where Raf and Shanah had hidden the Raithe steeds. And those I knew as I knew the garden at Fallowden.

I looked inside my memory and followed the way which she would have traveled to arrive there, and I could feel the light touches that were the thoughts of my two companions, keeping me company. Suddenly I found myself caught up in what seemed a wind of the spirit and borne off, across the valley we sat in, over the mountains, and I looked down upon Fallowden as it fled beneath, upon the grasslands, and then upon the toes of the mountains as they thrust out into the flatlands.

I knew then that I had been carried upon the strength of Tisha and Cara, drawing upon those powers which they possessed. But they had said that my own might would aid them, so I held the thought of my sister, and moved with them toward her hiding place.

There was a glimmer below us, as though of a campfire. Then our speed slackened, and we settled gently toward the spot. I could see a figure sitting before the flames, chin in hand, as I had seen Ruthella sit so many times before. My heart cried out to her, and it seemed that she heard it, for she straightened and look about as though seeking the source of a sound. Then Tisha spoke into her spirit, and all of us were linked as one.

"Ruthella, my child, I am a friend. My daughter and I bear with us, upon our spirits' backs, your brother Perrin. Long have you sat here among the horses, wondering how you might aid your own, if any still survive, to work against your enemy. And the time has come. Shanah is in the hands of the Tyrant's men, who bear her speedily toward Lirith. We will, with the aid of Those Who Wait, slow them somewhat in that journey.

"Raf works in the southern heights with an army of angry folk who have been ill-used by Him Who Sits at Lirith. They are well-armed and deadly fighters, but they have no steeds to give them speed in their arrival at Lirith, whereto they must hurry to arrive soon after Shanah. Your task is vital. You must collect the Raithe horses—all that are trained for riding—and hasten to the south. Follow the old trails that are marked with carven stones, avoiding all roads. When you come within sight of the snow peaks, then watch always for the stones in the shape of a bird with wings outspread. Raf will be upon that trail, moving to meet you, for we next must join our spirits to his and show him the pattern that moves upon the loom of Kyrannon.

"Should any misfortune overtake you, send your spirit's

cry upon the wind. For Shanah's child and the hermit Lengalyon sit upon the northern mountains, and they will surely hear you and find aid for you."

"Know that I will do what may be done," replied that which was my sister. "And happy am I to know that so many of my folk still walk in flesh upon the earth."

There was a slight tremor—no, it was more like a jolt or jar—and we sat again upon the settle in Tisha's kitchen. The blaze upon the hearth was not yet flickering out.

Narrative of Raf dir Raithe

For many weeks I labored among the folk of the mines, forging them into an army which none might be ashamed to field. Their smiths worked the glowing metal in their forges, hammering out sword and arrow-quarrel, shield and spearhead, until we were equipped, it might well be, far better than the troops of the Tyrant. Doshan himself claimed that he had never seen weaponry so well-worked and flawless.

Little did I think to find one so valuable as Doshan among the folk of this hidden height. The ways of the army he knows as he knows his own breath, the strategies which the lords employ formed the games of his childhood. And he knows Lirith as only the Sergeants of the Gates can ever know that city. Within himself he is an army.

One worrying thought nibbled at my heart. We were ready to move; in this we all agreed. Thonar said that it rested upon my judgment. Yet how might I know what passed beyond the mountains? One stroke we would have, chancing all upon its effectiveness; but I felt that others also were moving upon the path we trod, and I hesitated to commit our might until I found how best it could be done. Doshan also counseled patience. Even

Tathira, who speaks so seldom that all listen closely when she chooses to open her lips, said that she felt that we would be given a sign when the time ripened.

So we waited, but we never slacked our efforts to grow stronger, faster, more accurate with bow and sword and spear. Our armory we moved down the mountain to a secure hiding place, that we might not be slowed by such work when the time came to move.

Weeks passed with awful slowness, giving me time to think, which was ill work for me. Shanah and the child haunted my dreams by night and my thoughts by day, if I were not busied about some necessary task. But I held myself in patience and kept a cheerful face.

There came a night when I could not sleep. I had been quartered in the house of Doshan and Tathira, much to our mutual pleasure. Often I found Doshan wakeful in the night and talked the moons down with him before we sought our couches. Yet this night he slept. I could hear the heavy burring of his snores mixed with Tathira's light breathing as I passed their door.

Something drew me forth beneath the stars, which prickled their way through the needled branches of the great trees that ringed the village. I looked up, letting the peace of those far planets and suns sink into me. But there was a message abroad in the wind!

I moved, almost without volition, toward the keep where Thonar lay. Things were in motion, I could feel it as a deep vibration along my bones. With Thonar to link his spirit with mine, we might seek abroad for that which moved in the night.

Light glimmered beneath his door, and I knew that he

was as wakeful as I. He opened to my light tap, smiling to see me.

"There is work for us, this night, Kinsman," he said. "Something there is that speaks to those of our blood. Let us go out into the open and listen for its words."

So we went into the edge of the forest and sat upon the moss-smoothed roots of a giant tree. Leaning our backs against the bole, we linked hands and closed our eyes. And they were there, inside our hearts, three beings who had sought for us across the lands. One of them was Perrin.

"My brother!" I cried in my thought. "Good it is to know you safe."

A gentle presence made answer. "And we, who thought to find one Raithe are allowed by the gods to find two. A generous gift, indeed.

"Know you, my friends, that Perrin cannot speak with you, though he knows what you say to us. He is only now finding that he has gifts of the spirit. We have found your sister Ruthella, and she comes from the grasslands bringing the Raithe horses for your use. Well it is that you have waited upon the mountains, for all might have been lost had you moved too soon. Now you must go, and swiftly, to meet your sister; then, with the steeds to lend you speed, to Lirith, for there Shanah will be taken before you can arrive."

My heart gave a terrible bound within me. "Shanah goes there?" I cried; "is she then in the hands of the Tyrant?"

"Not yet," soothed the voice in my spirit. "Though his men hold her captive, they will do her no harm, for their orders have been sternly given. No Raithe is to come to any unnecessary hurt but is to be brought straightaway into the presence of Him Who Sits at Lirith. And that bringing will not be so smooth nor so quick as one might think.

"For I, Tisha, and my daughter, Cara, and your brother Perrin have gone out into the grasslands and called abroad to Those Who Wait. They knew us without delay, for they are all spirit, unfettered by the limiting flesh. The ways toward Lirith are now guarded, and though Shanah's captors hold desperately to their purposes, still they will be hindered again in their journeying."

Then Thonar asked reflectively, "Are we to strike at Lirith, with our limited strength, and free Shanah?"

Tisha laughed. "There will be no great need of prolonged attack by arms. For we have sought far for counsel, and farther still, and the Initiates in the Tower of Truth, which stands at the edge of the Purple Waters by the city of Shar-Nuhn, have heard our cry. Our best weapon, so they have affirmed, is that which is within our spirits. And so will the Tyrant be stricken, if we succeed. But success will bring the need for ordering the realm and the city of Lirith, and for that we shall need armed might. For this purpose only the gods have brought forth an army out of the mines of the south.

"And, Raf dir Raithe, it is your son, whose days may only be added into weeks, who stands as the anchor and might of that link which holds for us the Initiates' aid. No such spirit ever has been known in Kyrannon—or elsewhere, if I am not wrong. Ashraf, his mother has named him, and he sits in the lap of Lengalyon upon the northern heights. They two, unaided, strove across the long ways to Shar-Nuhn, and they two will serve as the funnel through which the might of all the Initiates will be channeled into those who strive with the Tyrant."

Again my heart bounded, but this time it was for joy. My son . . . only now did the reality of his existence come to me. He lived and was united, even at so tender an age, with those who serve the gods.

"Time is our friend, if we do not waste it. But it will be our enemy if we are laggards," whispered the spirit of Tisha into my listening heart. "Go to meet your sister, and know that the work of the gods is in our hands. The long fate of Kyrannon trembles upon the lip of time."

Thonar laughed aloud. "For this have we stayed our hands, waiting for a sign. And you have brought us comfort beyond all our hope, Lady. Have no fear for our part. We are ready to move within this hour."

"My thanks to you, Friend Tisha, and to your daughter and my brother. We shall outrun the river to the lowlands," I said, and I felt a light touch upon my hand, as though a small hand had been laid there.

Then they were gone, and Thonar and I stood, unkinking our bones, then hurried into the village, calling aloud to the people to come forth. And before the stars upon the western sky were set the army had moved forth to stand beside the arms cache, and I had gone far down from the height, racing to meet Ruthella and those horses of silver and smoke which were a part of the blood of all Raithes.

The journey that had been measured in weeks, for me, was now cut to days, so great was our haste. By the old

roads we went, following stones marked with symbols so
ancient that the washing of rain and the beating of hail
had all but effaced them. And almost every night the
three travelers-in-spirit found us where we were camped
and relayed to Thonar and to me the progress of the great
coming-together that was converging upon Lirith.

They were, themselves, journeying in haste across the
grasslands to meet with us and with Ruthella, that we
might all arrive at one time before the walls of the city.
Only Lengalyon and the child were not moving. They sat
upon the mountain before their fire, and the force of
many spirits was channeled through their minds, for the
gods were at work among us, using our capacities and
strengths as strands upon their tremendous looms.

There came a day when my captive horse, which now
we used as a pack-beast, threw up his head and whinnied
joyfully. In my heart I felt a stirring of recognition, and I
ran ahead of Doshan and Thonar to reach the top of a
hillock that rose before us. In the brook-hollow that lay
behind it there was movement, and I saw with joy that
the distant reaches were filled with shapes of smoke and
silver, as the horse-herd of Fallowden raced toward the
water.

I threw up my hand and gave the long hail that was
the call of our family, and a well-loved voice answered
me from the distance. Then Lindfal, that great stallion
upon whose back the Raithe had last ridden, broke free
from the herd, and I saw that Ruthella rode him, though
more awkwardly than was her wont. As she drew near, I
saw with joy that she was great with child, and I cried to
her, "Our beloved Millis left his seed upon the soil of our

lands. My heart is happy to see you, Sister, and happy also to see your dear burden."

Then Lindfal reached the hillock and, stepping carefully, as though he knew the value of his passengers, brought Ruthella to my side. She slid from his bare back into my arms, and we stood for a time without words, taking comfort from our embrace.

Now the miner-folk were arriving about us, and great was their astonishment at the splendor of the beasts that awaited them.

"Few of my people are horsemen," Thonar said to me, "but we will learn quickly, for our need is great. By the time the three from the west come to this place, most of us will ride well enough to travel, and the journey to Lirith will give practice enough for all."

That evening, we devised blanket-and-strap saddles, bridles of thongs and rope, and stirrups made of bits of metal brought for repairing weapons. In the morning, the grasslands about were filled with unsteady riders and patient horses who were learning the ways of one another. By nightfall great progress had been made; and on the third day, when Tisha, Cara, and Perrin came from the west, the army was mounted, more or less at ease, on the horses of Raithe.

Now there was need of great haste, said Tisha, and we must move toward Lirith at top speed. Even nightfall did not halt us, for we rode by moonlight, Ralias, the lesser moon, being near the full. When we camped at last for a few drugged hours of sleep, I knew that Tisha and Cara still moved abroad in spirit, as they did whilst riding, carrying on the work of the gods. They were filled with strength that amazed me, but Perrin reassured my heart, saying that they were drawing upon the energies of others who were far away. No harm would come to them, he promised, and I slept more easily in the security of his words.

Now we drew near to Lirith, and patrols began to sight us. None escaped to bring the word to Lirith, for no horse bred by the townsmen could outdistance our steeds, and we held many prisoners, long before the walls of Lirith came into view. We came at noon upon the unsuspecting city, and the gates were barred against us, as the drums thrummed upon the walls and the people shouted and milled about, seeking to enter the sally-ports.

We sent no emissary and raised no cry. Our lines formed beyond arrow-shot of the wall, and we sat our mounts, waiting for a signal from gods or men. For an hour we sat, and though the sun was blazing down, the rest was welcome.

Then came a clamor on the walls, and the gates opened wide enough to let through a file of horsemen. Their lances glittered in the afternoon light, and their shields were blazoned with the emblems of many old and noble families. At the same time, archers took their places along the walls, and we signaled to our own bow-women to deploy to right and left, taking cover behind rocks and low-growing bushes. My signal brought from them a flight of arrows that cleared the wall, much to the surprise of those within the city. Our bows are better than theirs, as Doshan attests, and our women stronger than most of their men.

As our arrows passed over them, the troop before the

gate charged, and others streamed from the opening behind them to follow them against us.

Doshan blew into his great ram's horn, and the guttural boom of its voice echoed from the city walls. Our lines stood firm, lances ready, swords shining dangerously in the blazing sunlight. Then I set my heels into Lindfal's sides, and he leaped forward. I raised my sword and shouted, "The Raithe! The Raithe!"

We thundered down to meet the Tyrant's men, and it was close work with swords, after the lances shattered or were lost in the flesh of men. Many a time I turned to find a swordsman who had threatened my back sinking with a feathered shaft piercing his armor. And many a time I looked into the eyes of one whom I must slay, my heart weeping that this must be.

Amid the clamor and the dust, the clang of swords and the whinnies of horses, I heard, at last, a voice speaking inside my heart.

"Now the gods have completed their pattern."

So spoke Tisha, and at that moment a cloud, where there had been no cloud, passed over the sun's face, darkening the plain in one instant to twilight.

There came a pause, as all who fought felt the chill of that shadow pass across their hearts. I heard Thonar cry, "Have done! Wait upon the gods!" And there came a silence upon the fields, broken not even by a groan from the dying.

Narrative of Him Who Sits at Lirith

Never was there one so badly served as I in all the days of Kyrannon. Those who command my forces, those who are sent to do my bidding in simple things that hold little danger, even those to whom I entrust my secret thought— all are incompetent.

Tharan I had held to be warrior-bred and true to my interests. The command of all my cavalry I gave him, then sent him upon this trifling quest into the grasslands. And he returned with a bare third of the force he took into the field with him, no new horses, and less than half of the mounts which his troops had ridden forth.

Truly I was mistaken in his tempering, though under the questioning he never varied his tale, incredible though it was. Even on the third day, when he was half in delirium, he hung in the chains and stared at me with half-blind eyes, still wailing of Those Who Wait upon the lands about Fallowden.

Nothing could be gained by questioning the troopers. The sergeants answered dutifully, but their words conveyed nothing, and the men claimed utter ignorance of the causes of their rout. And the horses shivered in their stalls, their eyes rolled back still in terror. What strange army could have met such a force within the bounds of our own country and vanquished them without leaving tales of their coming and going along the track of their march?

Know that I was not satisfied to leave this dishonor unanswered. Another force was readied, and to this commander I gave stern orders. He must return with either horses or Raithes, if any still should live. If he did not, his own head would rot upon the gatepost. His family would be scourged forth from the city to starve in the southern swamps. His house would be burned to the ground and his animals slain. Harsh measures, you may say, but one who rules must oftentimes use stern measures, that the public good may be served.

So they went forth again into the grasslands, and I waited with little patience for word to be brought to me. Day followed day, and no messenger approached the city from the west. My sleep was broken by ill dreams, and once I even found myself doubting my own purposes; a thing which I have prided myself upon avoiding.

No, I must not doubt my aims. But I am well-warned. If such as this is the performance of my army in time of peace, what catastrophe might have befallen had I sent them forth for conquest untried! Untiring effort must I now exert, forcing the training, the hardening of all those under my sway. Not only those who served under arms, but the common folk must deny themselves rest and ease, luxury and even necessity. All must bend to the wind of my purpose; forget their selfish aims in the higher goals which I would set before them.

Some weeks passed, and the city sweltered in the summer sun, while the citizens labored upon the walls and toiled in the quarries, building defenses. For though we would go against those who did not expect us, nevertheless only a fool will not give thought to reverses of fortune. Should the attacked seek to become the attacker, we should be secure.

In the midst of this turmoil, a rider came from the west bearing news. Though not that which I desired, yet his message was welcome. A Raithe was taken and would be brought before me as quickly as might be done. I rewarded the man with a gold piece and questioned him further. Then I went into my chambers to think upon his words.

It might well be, I mused, that the taking of one of the Raithe women would be the key that turned this stubborn lock. Most likely, the men were adamant folk, hard to crack in the jaws of truth. But a woman would be easier to manage. From her I would acquire the information I needed. And with her as a tool, I should pry loose from those miserly lands the horses I must have. The messenger had insisted that the captive was both young and comely. "Not what we'd call a beauty," he had said, "but well enough for such a tall, dark girl. And strong. Four it took to capture her, and then only after striking her senseless with a sword-hilt. Had it been one-to-one, she would have gone free, they told me."

Well. Such strength! I discounted it, of course, for common men always wish to seem more than they are and exaggerate the smallest incident into heroic proportions in order to build up their own prowess. Nonetheless, she likely had struggled with them, in her poor and inept fashion, and I would do well to congratulate them upon their capture of this dangerous enemy. It might even be wise to watch her and to see that no weapon came to her hand. I had known women to seek, in the hysteria of anger or grief, to set blade in my flesh.

So I set myself to await the arrival of this Raithe, curious to see what sort of folk they were in truth, unmagnified by the lens of fear and rumor. But I waited long. The messenger had said that a week would see the troop at my door, but it did not come. At length I sent him forth again to find what kept them upon the road, but he never returned to Lirith. Such was his ingratitude, though I had favored him and rewarded him well.

Yet the end of the second week brought a cry from the wall. Dust was within eyeshot, and the force was returning with the captive. I washed myself and donned fine robes, for I find that often persuasion does more to sway a woman than does threat. And if she were comely . . . who knows? I was not averse to taking a new favorite when it suited my purpose.

The woman they brought before me was a surprise—I will admit it. No such had I ever seen before. Tall she stood, as a warrior would, ignoring the dust of the road that coated her skin and her hair, undismayed by the ugly gray robe that she wore. Only her eyes lacked dust, and they were glittering black and alive, though they seemed not to take note of me or of anything within my chamber.

Then I understood. She would be weary past belief, no doubt, and perhaps still suffering the effect of her knock upon the head. I smiled as gently as a father upon her and said, "Welcome, my child, to Lirith. You are overcome with weariness, I know, and would clean yourself.

These ladies who attend me shall take you to the pools, where you may rest yourself and bathe. Fresh raiment will be brought to you. Compose yourself and feel secure. I shall send for you presently."

Such a fair speech surely might have gained gratitude. Yet I caught a skeptical glint in those dark eyes and a curious quirk to her full lips that seemed to say that she understood what I meant and not what I said. But that, of course, was quite impossible. What barbaric maiden, raised among horses and wild men, could ever hope to see through the wiles of a polished courtier?

Still, I went about my morning tasks with more than a little unease. What had there been in her eyes? She had stood before me as though she were the ruler and I the captive. No sense of peril surrounded her. She had walked from the chamber in perfect confidence. Of what was she confident? The question troubled me.

When noon was at hand, I sent after my house-mistress and asked after the woman.

Lalith laughed. "Such poise was surely wasted in the outland. She bathed herself and washed her hair. Then she fell asleep as sweetly as a babe at breast. Only lately did she rouse and ask that we bring her tunic and trousers instead of the gown you had chosen for her. Should we do as she asks?"

Anger that she had scorned my choice stirred at my heart. Then I smiled. "Give her what she wishes, and when she is clad, bring her to me."

When she stood again before me, it was with the same insolent grace that I had sensed before. Yet I hid my displeasure and invited her to sit. She chose a high-backed chair which faced my own, and she leaned her head against the cushion and surveyed me from head to foot, as I had thought to scan her. To judge from her expression, she was not favorably impressed.

Now I was truly angry. "You might do well to seek to please me," I told her severely. "There are those of your blood, no doubt, still at large upon the countryside. When they fall into my hands, as surely they shall, your conduct toward me could count heavily for or against them."

Then she laughed—not loudly, but with much amusement. "Little do you know, Tyrant, with what forces you contend," she said. "You see one woman, yet you do not truly see her. Why, I wonder? What is there within you that cannot know the truth, however it comes to you? How many men, I wonder, have you tortured to their latter ends, seeking truths that they gave you freely before?"

I thought of Tharan, and a little chill ran down my back. But no, such ravings as his could never be truth. I sat straighter and looked as stern as my face would allow.

"Levity is not the part of wisdom, when you are captive to a king," I said.

"Oh, now you are a king?" she asked brightly. "And do the folk of Lirith know this, or do you seek to astonish them?"

I rose. "In time Kyrannon will become an empire. I shall sit at its summit, and you might sit nearby, if you sought to please me. You might begin by telling me the whereabouts of those great horses which are the fame of your house."

"As quickly would I tell you the whereabouts of my son," she answered. "Know, Tyrant, that there are, as you say, those of my blood still in flesh upon the lands about. And the least of them, who is my son Ashraf, is greater than you as the sun is greater than a candle-flame. You are beset, Tyrant. Though you may not yet be aware of it, you harbor your nemesis within your walls."

I leaned above her, caught her by the throat, shook her. Her strong hands closed over mine and pried my fingers loose. She stood and thrust me down into the chair where she had sat. Though I am a man fully large as any, and though I am strong, among my own kind, she moved me as though I were a child.

Then she bent over me, and her hair swung, black and silky, over her shoulders and touched my cheek. I looked up, straining against her hands, and I saw her eyes.

Closer, they came, and closer. I looked into her eyes!

Part III:

The Pattern Is Completed

Narrative of Shanah ni Raithe do Raithe

Safe upon the northern heights I sat, with Lengalyon and my son for company. Yet my heart roamed the lands below, seeking for Raf, for my folk. And truly, I could not sense in my inner knowing that all were lying dead at Fallowden. Something there was inside my spirit that still glowed with the life that was my husband. Something there was in my veins that felt the living selves that were my kin. And something there was that told me of the movements of Those Who Wait upon the lands beneath.

As my strength returned I could not contain myself within a hole, however safe. I felt the need to be up and doing, stretching myself against the mountain heights, tempering my muscles to their old hardness, my eyes and hands to their accustomed skills. In the clean chill of those heights I strove against winds and stones and perilous passages, and I left the aching bitterness of that last day at Fallowden, drop by drop, with my sweat and my blood there in the laps of the gods.

And I found not only my body renewed. Though I had never sought within myself for trace of those talents which were Talitha's, yet I found some sense of them within me. Lying against the sun-warmed rock, I might close my eyes and force my spirit outward, little by little, over long days and weeks, seeing first the grassblades about my own feet, then the deer that moved in the forest a few rods distant. Outward I pushed my sensing, until I could look abroad into the grasslands.

Each time my son ventured into my thought, I found my powers made greater. The stream that ran between Ashraf and Lengalyon became visible to me, though I said nothing to the hermit, feeling raw and unready in the face of his great abilities. But I persisted, and a day came when I inched my way up the sheer face of rock at the mountain's peak, seeing only with the inward eye. Then I knew myself to be more than I had been, and I rejoiced to have this new gift to bring to Raf, when again we met.

There came a day when I lay behind a stony outcrop, looking away down the grasslands toward Fallowden, which was hidden past the curve of the world. I was drowsy after long exertion and warm with the sun, and my spirit was open as that of any babe to sending from outward. And such there came.

Within my thought there moved another, and alien, thought; yet I felt kinship with it. My whole self focused upon it, and I held myself alert, though still relaxed in every bone. The thought moved again, growing stronger, and I recognized its source.

That tender and wistful attention I had felt before, when Those Who Wait had led me forth to safety and shelter from Fallowden. Even such concern as this had surrounded me as I birthed Ashraf in the grasslands, long weeks ago. Those of my kind were about me, invisible even as shadows in the strong sun of summer, but there to my sensing. I waited upon their message, for such I knew that they must bear.

"Shanah of the Raithe," they whispered to my heart, "There is work sent by the gods for your hand to grasp. Aid will come from afar, though it is not yet called. But your time is now. Men of the Tyrant move upon this mountain, up the southern slopes, seeking for any they may find who are Raithe. They must not find your son, for his task will be other. You they must find and bear to Lirith. Such, our spirits tell us, will aid the gods in their working out of the destinies of men in Kyrannon.

"Go not willingly, but fight them as you would if taken unaware. Do not call with your spirit to Lengalyon. Only set yourself in their path so that they may find and over-power you.

"Such is the message we bring you from the gods, who have us in care. Go in joy, knowing yourself to be a tool which will be sharpened even more as you move toward Lirith. Hold your heart open to sendings from afar. The weaving of the gods is moving into its pattern, and you are a shining weft therein."

The touch faded, and I lay for a moment, setting myself to this strange task. Then I rose and sped toward the forests that crowned the southern slopes, seeking with my newfound powers to find where the men moved and upon which path I might encounter them. But they walked upon no path, but followed our horses as they made their way from the grasslands. Fearing to set their feet into traps, the men stumbled through the rough forest, cursing and seeking to keep Gollas and Wandir and Plana within their view.

A shiver touched me. With what intricate care did the gods move their creatures across the warp of their weaving. If my longfathers were correct, and I could not feel them in error, this too was a part of the pattern; that our steeds should seek us out, leading those who were unwitting tools of the gods into the place where they must be. With such hands guiding destiny, I could find no fear in my heart, only a singing and fierce joy that I might again loose sword in sheath against the henchmen of the Tyrant.

I laid the angle of my approach on a diagonal across their direction, feeling certain that one of the four would detect my presence. I walked freely, as one who feels herself secure in a secret place. It was difficult to seem unaware of them, but I was caught up on the shuttles of the gods and I did not falter nor steal a sidewise glance. When the first leaped from the thickets before me, I halted and shouted aloud, then drew my sword and dropped into a crouch.

They must breed a slack sort of woman in the towns. They approached as though to take the blade from an unresisting hand. The first man felt my blade slip between his ribs and stared down at his wound in astonishment. Him I could have slain, but I felt it not a part of the pattern, so I only disabled him, then turned to the others.

That was a merry bout indeed. I had never battled against three swordsmen at one time, and it was an illumination to the mind in the many possibilities of swordplay. My blade tasted blood from all the three remaining, but he whom I had wounded returned to the fray and seized me from behind. Then I kicked out heartily, butting backward with my head and jabbing with my elbows. Almost, I won free, but one must have crept up behind, where I could not see, for there came a ringing blow against my skull, and I slid slowly into darkness.

Even as I slipped away into that blackness, I felt in my heart a terrible outcry, and I knew that my son had known of my plight and that his young spirit felt itself cut loose from the anchor that a mother must be to her youngling. I sought to send from my dimming self a reassurance, but there was no time, and I knew nothing more for long.

I woke to darkness which was touched with firelight. For a time, I did not stir nor fully open my eyes but lay glancing through slitted lids about the encampment. A large force was upon the plains, for many campfires were dotted about. I could see the shadows that were men sitting or moving about. To observe those nearby, I must turn my head, and this I did, after a time, opening my eyes fully and sighing.

At once, a stocky young man in the cloak of an officer was beside me, standing with hands hooked into swordbelt, gazing down at me. I struggled to sit, but my hands were too tightly bound to give aid, so I turned upon my side.

"Well, toad of Him Who Sits at Lirith," I said. "You seem to have made a dangerous catch. One lone woman you will take back to Lirith?"

He laughed—a short bark holding no amusement. "Had I not found you, Lady, I should have found my head upon the northern gate, communing with the carrion birds. The First Minister said to me, 'Bring me a Raithe or horses, and if none are to be found, bring me your head.' You will do well enough. For there are none of your kin to be found, though not all died at Fallowden. No horse have we seen, save those my troopers followed up the mountain—and they melted as the snows of spring into the forest and have been seen no more. You will serve my purpose well, and my thanks to you for my life. Your fate at the hands of the First Minister I will not think on. But you shall suffer no harm at my hands nor those of my men. If you will bind yourself in honor not to seek escape, I shall free your hands and feet."

"You are courteous, and I cannot blame a soldier who performs his task. I so bind myself," I replied, and he knelt and severed my bonds. Then I rose with some difficulty, and he led me to the fire, where a pot of stew simmered.

Fed and washed, I felt more like Shanah ni Raithe, and I laid myself down upon the good blanket which he offered me and fell into slumber at once. And into that sleep there came a force, working upon my thought, my spirit, my whole being. There were voices there, giving direction to my actions, and there was a molten fury of energy which seemed to melt from me all weakness, all unease. It filled me to the brim with powers which I could neither recognize nor control, but one voice rose above the others and soothed my misgivings.

"Each night upon the road, each day as you travel, we shall be with you, teaching you the ways we know. The forces which you harbor come from many sources, and you must be tutored in their uses. Those Who Wait will provide the time for your teaching. And know you that I am Cara, also a young woman, and I am new-made wife to your brother Perrin. So we are sisters in fact as in spirit. This will bind us into a closeness which will help you to use my arts as your own. You go to do battle with Him Who Sits at Lirith, and I shall be your teacher."

I knew great peace. My brother lived and was wed to one with powerful arts. I was not alone, but united with a band of spirits of awesome potency. Truly, I was blessed by the gods to be sent as their weapon into the lair of the Tyrant.

Morning saw us upon the southern road, bound for Lirith. My captor, the Lord Heraad, watched me closely but treated me well, though he entrusted the rein of my mount to a sergeant, who rode ever beside me. Heraad set a swift pace, and I wondered if even the efforts of Those Who Wait might break the stern grasp which he maintained over his force.

Yet none of my blood, I believe, can know the full weight of sensation which comes to outlanders who listen for the first time to those doleful wails upon the wind. With the approach of noon, in the full sunlight of summer, with no wind to aid them nor snow to give them shape, they moved upon the cavalcade. Even I, who knew them to be my long kin, felt my flesh rise in ridges and my hair crickle upright at the roots, as they approached.

The horses went quite mad, flinging riders into the dust of the road and running away at heart-bursting speed into the grasslands. Men were in little better case, kneeling in the dust where they fell, holding their ears against the awful shrilling of the voices. Even Heraad was hard put

to hold his mount in check, and my sergeant disappeared
in a swirl of dust and curses. I held my steed firmly between my knees until I could gather up the dangling
reins. Then I leaned forward and spoke into his ear the
love-words we sing to our smoke-silver children. He
whiffled and stamped, but he stood his ground as though
he were one of our own stock.

Then I was puzzled as to my course. If I had no purpose in seeking out the Tyrant, I should even now be
fleeing. But I must not escape. I turned my horse and
made for the grasslands. Luckily, I found it difficult and
dangerous to seek speed over the ground that was littered
with men and equipment, so that it was not long before
Heraad himself rode to intercept me.

"You have met my kin, Lord Heraad," I said when he
caught the bit to halt my passage. "A Raithe dead is
rather more fearsome than one alive—do you not agree?"

He was blanched pale beneath the tan leather of his
cheek. "Such a strange tale did Tharan tell, upon his return from these accursed lands, that none believed it possible. He hangs in chains, near to death, in the Great
Keep at Lirith, babbling of Those Who Wait. Are these
they?"

"Truly," I said. "They guided me forth from the hands
of those who came to Fallowden with the spring, as they
have guided many generations of my folk in their peril.
And each stroke that is aimed at Fallowden increases
their number. They will harry you from here to the walls
of Lirith, for you bear with you one of their own. It will
require an uncommonly determined man to win through
their wall of terror, taking with him his men and his

mounts." I smiled confidently at him, and his pale eyes narrowed.

"Think not to escape, Lady Shanah. I would not bind you unless I must, but go with me you shall. Not only my own life will be forfeit if I return without you, but that of my wife and my younglings and my mother. Desperation can armor the joints of determination. Be warned," he said softly.

Then he turned and rallied his sergeants and his men and set them catching the horses and ordering the scattered supplies. No more distance could he hope to cover this day, I well knew, so I gave him my sworn word again and turned aside into the shadow of roadside trees to await orders. I closed my eyes to find my teacher again waiting for me. So I passed the afternoon, as dusty men clanked and swore about the roadside, seeking to renew their courage against another such assault as the noontide had brought.

By nightfall, a camp was set and in order, horses double-picketed, men braced against panic with generous gulps of wine. I slept again to the hum of voices inside my spirit, and I knew myself to be growing stronger with each hour.

The next dawn shone forth to find us again on the road, but our pace was deliberately slow. Heraad found that speed brought attack. So we proceeded slowly, for a time. By noon he was again ready to force the pace, but with his first order to trot, the long wails began to sound in the distance. He signaled the sergeants hurriedly and they slowed the column again to a walk. And so we made our way to Lirith, ambling upon the hot and dust-ridden way, unable to make speed.

Each night found my strength redoubled, my spirit more knowing, my heart fuller of joy. I soon found that my son's spirit was the force that aimed and bore that tide of thought to me. Others there were who could and would have done the task, but none so well as he, with so little effort. Upon his strength and Lengalyon's rested the weight of the sendings, and pride filled me that Raf and I had made such a child.

So the journey went, by slow stages, and I learned to master the strange energies that flickered within my spirit as thunderbolts flash in high-piled cloud. Excitement grew as we neared the city. I felt myself caught up in tremendous tides that bore me and Cara and Ashraf and all who labored with us as though we were chips afloat upon the great waters.

At last the wall of the city of Lirith lay upon the edge of sight, and Heraad dared to order the troop into a trot. One last wail bade us farewell, and we jostled and clanked and bumped our hasty way to the gates. A blast of noise greeted us, as all the drummers at the alarm drums began to pound upon their tub-shaped instruments. Amid the din, we entered into the city and were swallowed up in noise and clamor, as though all the fowl in the world were clacketing together. More men and women than I had ever thought or wanted to see all my life long were gathered about the streets, gabbling and pointing as we rode through. But they fell back when we neared the tall house that Heraad said was the dwelling of the First Minister.

They took me before the Tyrant, but so strong was the current coursing through me that I paid little heed to him or his trappings. But when he set a false smile upon his face and spoke with a sticky-sweet tongue, I looked at him, knowing his falseness all through with that glance. Those who saw through my eyes were adept at winnowing the truth from the souls of men, and they saw him as he was, in all his shoddy self-delusion. I turned from him, sickened, and followed the gaggle of women through the house to the bathing pools, there to cleanse the dust from my skin and the weariness from my bones.

Long I slept. When I woke, I found waiting for me a gown of fine stuffs, rich with laces and triflings, entirely unbefitting the tool of the gods. I asked the woman Lalith to find tunic and trousers for me, such being the proper raiment for a warrior. She laughed and looked at me with scorn in her eyes.

"Foolish girl. If he finds you well-favored, he may choose to raise you to his side, for a while. Fortune can attend one so placed. You could go forth, when he tires of you, with both your hands filled with jewels."

In turn, I laughed. "Know you, woman, that I am a warrior, of a warrior race. My folk hold honor above life, and wealth is not coveted by us. Gather what jewels you may for yourself, but allow me to walk my way unencumbered by such. Find me fit clothing, and I will attend upon your Tyrant."

She caught her breath and covered her mouth with her hand. "Never call him that!" she hissed. "Heads have been forfeited for such talk. Speak softly if you hope to continue to walk upon the grass and to feel the sun."

Then I knew her to be merely silly and not wicked, so I smiled and said again, "Do not concern yourself, but find me clothing."

So she went away and presently returned with what I sought, a long green tunic and darker green trews, which I donned gratefully. As she led me along the maze of passages, she looked back more than once with fear in her eyes. She was a small spirit, but not ill-disposed, and when we reached the heavy door that guarded the Tyrant, I touched her shoulder and said, "Go in peace, Lalith. None shall harm you, and you shall be cared for."

She shot me a startled glance and hurried away. Before I could touch the panels of the door, two armed men stepped from niches to either side and stood beside me. One rapped upon the door, and when the voice from inside called out, the other opened it.

I stepped inside alone and stood beside that tall, small man. His eyes held unease as he regarded me, and in a heartbeat he asked me to sit. Words passed between us then, but I attended little to them. My lips spoke that which was placed upon them, and as he answered and argued I could feel him grow angry.

The current within my spirit was pouring hotly now through all my being. I felt as though my eyes were glowing with fire to light the darkness, and my hands seemed to tingle with unexpended strength. Thus, when he bent above me and caught my throat in his hands, I thrust them aside as though he were no greater than Ashraf. I stood and took him in my hands and set him in the chair, and he looked up at me with terror in his eyes.

I bent over him, looking deep inside him, probing with

all the many powers that were moving through me. I caught his soul within that hot grasp and held it forth to the light, that he might see himself and his peers and all the world in the light of truth, which was burning inside my heart like a mighty torch.

"No," he croaked. "*No!*" He writhed in the chair, clawing at the arms. "Such cannot be truth. I will not have it so!"

At that moment, the drums upon the walls of the city began a thunderous uproar, and there came frantic knocking at the door that the Tyrant had so carefully barred behind me.

"Lord, we are attacked by a mounted host," came the cry, but he could not hear it. He was adrift in his own spirit, subject to the wills of Kla-Noh, of Tisha and Cara, of Lengalyon and Ashraf, of many whose names I did not know but whose spirits armored and reinforced my own.

The truth waxed hotter, and his spirit shriveled in that heat. We turned his soul's sight upon every act of his life, upon the truth of every word that he believed a lie and every lie that he had thought to be truth. Many a tortured face swam through his memory, crying out facts that he had spurned. Many a betrayal he recalled, done for his high purposes, as he had thought, but in actuality whims and caprices of his error-ridden heart. We felt his pain. We felt his spirit turning in the flame which held it. Pain was in us all, but we persisted.

And about the city of Lirith, with one part of our inner sight, we could sense a turmoil of horses and of armed men and women who charged the defenders before the walls beneath a curtaining shower of arrows that rained over the wall into the packed host within. On the plain before the gate, horsemen battled horsemen, and the flashing of their steel blades flickered even through the haze of agony that the soul of the Tyrant spread through our hearts.

"Have done!" I cried at last. "There is no more Tyrant in the great chair at Lirith. Look upon this shrunken thing. He will look no more abroad into the affairs of his neighbors, seeking to squeeze their wealth into his coffers. Now, and for as long as he lives, he stares into his own heart, and that vision is a burden and a woe."

The tide lessened, the heat cooled. I felt sad acquiescence from many sources, and the voice of Cara spoke inside me. "With his changing, there would have been unrest in all Kyrannon, struggles for his power, connivings and conspiracies. But the gods have wrought better than this. There is an army at the gates of Lirith. Even now the defenders are fleeing the walls, and the great gate is beset. Now you must bear him up from his torment, for a space, that he may order the gates opened, so that none may die without need. One whom you will joy to see rides at the head of those who will enter. Take this poor creature by the hand and force him to do the one good which he can achieve for his country."

So I took the hand of the man in the chair and lifted him to his feet. He looked up at me with abstracted eyes and sought to turn away, but I led him forth from his door.

The guards in the hall rushed forward, weapons in

hand. "What has befallen you, Lord?" they cried. "We called for you, and you did not hear!"

I forced words through his stiffened lips, "I am well enough, though weary. I have been visited by the gods, and they have given me a sign. Go out and open the gates to those without.

"They have been sent by the gods, though it may seem strange to you that they come thus, armed and fierce. I have seen new portents and been given signs that cannot be ignored. There will be change now." He turned and walked back into his chamber, and I waited at the slitted window, watching down the street as the gatehouse guards wound the chains upon the spindles, slowly wrenching open the gates of the portal.

The tumult without had quieted, and the waiting army was mounted upon Raithe horses! My heart slowed with wonder, then leaped as I saw who led the van. Raf rode through the gates, and I bounded through the window and dropped softly to the street, then ran to meet him. Behind him was Ruthella, and there was another whom I knew to be of us, though unknown to me.

I was swept up behind Raf, onto Lindfal, who had borne the Raithe upon his back. We rode into the city, and the folk were quiet, watchful, doubtful, and puzzled. I looked down at them with pity. They had been hardly used for long, yet how could they know that deliverance came with us?

I drew upon those new talents I possessed. I felt Raf join with me and knew that he also shared. Then I felt joy through all my being, and I sent it into that throng, washing over the despair and the doubt as would a wave from the sea.

Joy! Joy! Joy! And the faces relaxed, the hands unclenched. The people began to smile.

Narrative of Tisha

In my valley, the moon-trees drop their leaves once again. But my house waits for me, for still I dwell in Lirith, sitting in the foetor of the city, aiding those whom I love to bring order and peace to this land.

No longer does a tyrant sit in the great chair in the House of Justice. No longer do the cries of the tortured ring from the Great Keep. Only a subdued man of middle age rules here now, and he is so filled with pain that he may not bring pain to any other. Those who might seek to lay hand upon his office, now that he is no longer the stern lord that he was, must be quelled and brought to understanding, before we may put aside this weary task and return to our own ways and places.

How strange it is that we, who shun the populous places, must now make straight the paths of those who crave the jostle of cities and the voices of men. Yet Raf and Shanah labor beside Cara and Perrin, bringing this weft of the gods to a fitting conclusion. The people stand with us, however, and Doshan, that amazing man, has brought the forces of arms to our backs.

Two there are who aided him. Tharan, that unfortunate one who was sent against Fallowden, has survived his ordeal and stands as a terrible example of the justice dealt by the old order. Never a cruel man, he has been so tempered by his fate that he is far wiser than his years might warrant. He it was who upheld Doshan in his efforts to win over the armies.

As did Heraad. That lord, who worked in the pattern set by the gods, was not blind. Cara and I, to begin, and Those Who Wait taught him a stern lesson, and he watched with knowing eyes the working out of the weaving of Kyrannon. Now he labors with us, and, as he is an intimate of the great and the powerful, he is able to reach their ears and their hearts better than may we. His words hold weight for them, and his reputation for truthfulness stands us in good stead.

But many there are who must be sought out in the citadels of their hearts and made, by our arts, to see the things to which they have been wilfully blind. This is the task set to the hands of us who work with the spirit. And in this we have aid.

Lengalyon and Ashraf now dwell at Fallowden, whither they were brought by Ruthella from the northern heights. For that determined lady, though great with child, insisted upon returning to her home to set it in order against the return of Shanah and Raf. There, she insisted, should be the home of her nephew and his guardian, to bear her company until the family should be reunited.

From so near we may draw upon the strength of those two, who make a combination of powers unknown before in the annals of our kind. And the laughter of the child sounds through our hearts in odd seasons, for he finds the doings of his elders full of mirth. Often we pause in our serious occupations, hearing that irrepressible chime, and look again at the things which we find so gloomy and portentous. They are, we must admit, frequently ridiculous, and all our worryings aimed at the wrong target. Such a monitor keeps us balanced and cheerful.

Thonar has returned to his mines with his people. I often smile at the strange contrast those folk posed against the softer people of the city. Men stared in wonder at the men and women, alike under arms, clad alike, laboring alike, who seemed such comradely friends in their work. I have seen women of the town gazing after their stronger sisters with envy, and I should not wonder if a seed of thought has been set that may grow into a worthy plant, in times to come.

Though still we may call upon them at need, the Initiates have relaxed their constant watch upon us, and Kla-Noh, that sharp old fellow, has returned to his studies. Sometimes at night, when sleep evades me, I send a call into the night. If he is awake, we laugh over the day's happenings and wonder about the yesterdays and the tomorrows we will never know. We find great comfort together, and such a friend is a warmth in the chill of coming age. It would be well if he were of an age to set out upon a new adventure, for Initiates are coming to Kyrannon, at our urging, to set up a Tower of Truth, that the coming generations may be taught wisely. But he insists that his bones are too stiff and painful and his heart too closely attached to the folk of his own Tower for him to undertake such a task.

With the coming of the Initiates, we will be free to lay aside our tasks and return to our home. Cara and Perrin, as painfully as do I, long for that old stone house, for the strident call of the Grack, the twittering of the People of the Heights, the shy strangeness of the Wildings. Our hearts are there. There will my grandchildren grow in untrammelled joys and labors. Old Friend will go with us, for he seems to dream, in his stall, of his grass-patch and his Wilding kin. With us also will go three of the Raithe horses, that we may begin our own herd, for Perrin would never be content sundered from those four-hooved children of his folk.

But we shall be, always and ever, alert to the outside world. Never again will I shut myself away to save my own hurt. Linked into the skein of spirits that have wrought together in the name of the gods, we shall know what passes overmountain. Should another seek to take the Tyrant's place, he will find himself beset from south, from west, from north, by forces of terrible power. We go not to be hermits but free beings, living as we love to live.

So the pattern is completed, the shuttles return to their places, and the hands of the gods lie idle, or turn to other tasks.

If you enjoyed this Ace fantasy title, here is a sampling from another tale of magic and adventure by Ardath Mayhar, available from Ace Books in March, 1982:

The Seekers of Shar-Nuhn

This is Shar-Nuhn on the Purple Waters. Strong are the walls of Shar-Nuhn and deep her treasuries, for her fleets ply all the seas and gather riches for the canny Shar-Neen.

This is a city of secrets—small secrets, whispered in shadows; great secrets, hidden in temples. Secrets of wealth, secrets of crimes, secrets of conspirators, but in the city of Shar-Nuhn there are three secrets of paramount importance. The first of the Three Great Secrets teaches the seafarers of Shar-Nuhn to quiet the waters, in time of storm; wherefore no laden ship, no humble sailor of Shar-Nuhn is ever lost at sea.

The Second Secret is terrible truly, for it enables the Shar-Neen to trouble the lands to their foundations, as their enemies learned to their cost, in ages agone. Covetous eyes long envied Shar-Nuhn her riches, and an army marched forth for conquest. When the earth quaked and cracked before them, and their cities crumbled to rubble behind them, they turned up their eyes in despair and removed their place of abode, and sought no longer to trouble Shar-Nuhn.

But the Third Secret is a secret indeed, and none knows of it save the oldest of the Initiates in the Temple of Truth. Rumor says that is is the secret of illimitable wealth, or that it gives unending life and vigor, but there is only one who knows, and his life is dedicated to the preservation of the Third Secret of Shar-Nuhn.

Now there are those to whom the existence of a secret is a challenge—even a pain. It is an itch unscratched, a hunger unsatisfied. Such was the nature of Kla-Noh, the Seeker. Secrets had been his livelihood, for he purveyed his wares among the members of the Guild of Thieves, among the great merchants, among the wives and husbands of the rich. No secret was too poor and threadbare to arouse his interest. All were small itches, and he scratched them profitably. Naturally, the greater and more valuable the secret, the greater was the itch of Kla-Noh. And the Third Secret of Shar-Nuhn was the agony and the terrible unscratched itch of his life.

Though he knew well many of the Initiates, never would he ask of them. It would be worth much, in terms of wealth, to the Seeker who dared seek it in the Temple of Truth, but that was not the thing that tortured Kla-Noh. The thought of the secret itself tantalized him. To be the co-possessor of the Third Secret of Shar-Nuhn, having wrested it, unaided, from the Tower—surely there could be no higher aspiration for a Seeker After Secrets. To be able to fondle it in the private recesses of his mind, knowing that only one other on the planet could do the same, would be the finest sort of wealth for one like Kla-Noh. It would be a fitting climax and finale to his career, setting his seal upon his craft, as its one and unapproachable master. Then, and only then, could he retire to his modest villa and vineyard and spend his declining years sitting in the sun, considering the meanings of existence, probing into the questions that fill the universe, while the Purple Waters lapped the shore below his terrace.

On an evening in the dark of the moon, Kla-Noh descended his terrace to his small landing, got into his light sailing craft, and wafted gently across the curve of the bay to the harbor, where the great wharves lifted black bulks against the stars. Leaving his tethered craft dancing lightly upon the lipping wavelets, he made his way to a drinking place, where gathered the sailors and the harbor people. Kla-Noh sought a helper, for the Tower that was the Temple of Truth had been raised, by remarkable arts, from the floor of the sea and stood alone outside the protecting arm of the bay. One needed the aid of a man skilled in the arts of the sea, for the Purple Waters flung themselves strongly about the Tower of Truth, and any save the skilled found themselves swamped and sunk and drawn away into the mysteries of the sea.

There was a fair company at the Sign of the Dolphins, and Kla-Noh found a place in a shadowed corner and set himself to examine his companions. Most were bluff, wind-burned seamen with pale eyes, which seemed always to be looking into deep skies and boundless oceans. There were a handful of shopkeepers and clerks from the warehouses. At the long table beneath the window sat a grim-faced and red-haired young man, who wrapped his hands about his glass and gazed into it as if seeking the ends of all being therein. He was huddled in a ragged cloak, and his shoes were mere collections of holes. This man interested Kla-Noh, if for no other reason than that he had the look of one with secrets of his own, and any secret at all drew Kla-Noh like a magnet.

The Seeker bought a bottle of fair wine, then made his way to the long table and sat beside the man in the ragged cloak. After a lengthy moment, the ragged man's green eyes reluctantly left his glass and sought his unexpected companion. Something in the face of the Seeker seemed to amuse him, for he chuckled low in his chest.

"May I share your joke, my friend?" asked Kla-Noh. "And I shall gladly share with you my wine."

"Sit. Sit and be welcome, old man. You have the look of a Seeker. I, Si-Lun, have sought somewhat myself, and have a feeling for the craft." He moved down the stained bench, making room, and Kla-Noh poured generously from his bottle.

"You seem a stranger here," said Kla-Noh. "Shar-Nuhn can be more lonely than a star to a stranger without friends or family."

"All places are lonely to me, Seeker," answered the ragged man. "All lonely, alike, and all empty. The sea is my family and friend, my road and home."

The heart of Kla-Noh was touched, for he was a kindly man. And he thought, too, that one so ragged and rootless would be eager to help in his enterprise. His shrewd and withered features wrinkled in a smile, and he said to the ragged man, "If it will please you, I shall provide you with that which may substitute for family and friend, which will provide the home and make easier the road. And in return . . ."

"And in return . . ." echoed the man, and his eyes glowed greenly with strange laughter, and his lips twisted bitterly.

"I ask only your skill as a sailor, that is all. For one little hour—perhaps two. And if your old calling as a Seeker should urge you to aid me more, then I should welcome and reward such help."

Si-Lun looked deeply into his eyes, lifted his glass, and said, "I shall give you aid. Tell me your plan, that I may know what it is that I promise."

And Kla-Noh took him across the curve of the bay, to the landing where the waters lipped and lapped against the shore at the foot of his terrace. Deep into the night they sat beneath the wheeling stars, speaking softly in darkness, and now and again they would look far out, beyond the arm of the bay, where the Tower of Truth was only a speck of white light against the sea and the sky.

In a month, when again the moon rode below the horizon, they had completed their plan. A strongly ribbed dory bore them out of the bay and into the full surge of the Purple Waters. Si-Lun strove mightily with the oars, rowing them swiftly toward the Tower, as Kla-Noh sat, silent, thinking of the secret he longed to know.

Where the waters rolled and tumbled about the foot of the Tower, Si-Lun's skill was sorely tried, but he was adept, and he brought the dory to rest at last at the foot of the steps that led from the floor of the sea to the door of the Temple of Truth. There were those who said that, at times, the Initiates had been seen to descend those stairs and to disappear beneath the waters, as those who, descending a mountain, pass through a layer of cloud. None could say truly, for the ways of the Initiates are not the ways of mortal men.

But Si-Lun and Kla-Noh were not concerned with any tales save that of the Third Secret of Shar-Nuhn. They carefully tethered their dory, then made their silent way up the great stair to the door of the Temple. The door, as the law said it must, swung open to a touch, and Kla-Noh peered cautiously within. No voice, no footstep was to be heard. The spiraling stair rose into the silent Tower, and all the doors were closed upon the inner chambers. Yet the hall and the stair were brightly lit, for the law said that Truth must never stand in darkness.

So the two Seekers entered into the Tower and set their feet upon the stairway. And at the first doorway they stopped to read the writing upon the door. It said: "THIS IS THE CHAMBER OF THE FIRST SECRET, A QUIET SPELL, FOR THE USE OF SEAFARERS. ENTER, AND WELCOME." But they passed on.

Round and round they went, past the doors of the Initiates' chambers, and came to THE CHAMBER OF THE SECOND SECRET, A DANGEROUS DEVICE. SEEK COUNSEL BEFORE ENTERING. And they passed on.

Up they went, past rank after rank of closed doors, and came at last to a door across the stair, whereon was written: "CLIMB NO HIGHER IN THE TOWER OF TRUTH, FOR THAT WHICH LIES BEYOND CONCERNS NO MORTAL MAN." The door yielded to the touch.

Behind it stood a man.

The two Seekers looked upon him with awe and with dread, for his was a face scarred by long suffering, ravaged by unthinkable years. His eyes seemed to have looked upon nothing save agony and death, pain and torment.

He stretched out his hands before him and said, "The Creator of Truth has sent you at last to relieve me of my burden. It is written that, when the toll of the years grows too great upon the Oldest Initiate, there will be sent a substitute. The secret that you seek lies in the inner chamber. Go, either or both, and examine it. Yet I am required to tell you one thing. He who lifts the burden of the secret must bear it, as I have done, that I may go free. Each day I have gazed upon the workings of the secret. Each night I have meditated upon its purposes. Look upon my face: there you will see its reflection. Only death may erase its mark from me." He folded his hands in the sleeves of his robe and stood silent, under their gaze.

Long they looked upon him. Then Kla-Noh turned to Si-Lun, and each looked into the eyes of the other. With one accord, they went down through the Temple of Truth, got into their dory, and rowed away. Some itches, Kla-Noh realized, are better left unscratched.

—from *The Seekers of Shar-Nuhn*
by Ardath Mayhar